Walter Lowrie

Memoirs of the Hon. Walter Lowrie

Walter Lowrie

Memoirs of the Hon. Walter Lowrie

ISBN/EAN: 9783337388782

Printed in Europe, USA, Canada, Australia, Japan

Cover: Foto ©Andreas Hilbeck / pixelio.de

More available books at **www.hansebooks.com**

OF THE

HON. WALTER LOWRIE

EDITED BY HIS SON

NEW YORK

THE BAKER & TAYLOR CO.

5 AND 7 EAST SIXTEENTH STREET

1896

PREFACE.

THE first part of this book is a personal narrative —from Edinburgh, Scotland, to Butler, Penna., 1784 to 1810. The second part relates chiefly to public service—in the Legislature of Pennsylvania, the Senate of the United States, and as Secretary of the United States Senate—from 1811 to 1836. Included, according to its date in 1830, is a Treatise on Divine Revelation, presumably from Mr. Lowrie's pen. The third, and chief, part is based largely on the writings of Mr. Lowrie—reports, journals and correspondence ; and also on personal interviews and conversations with him as the Corresponding Secretary for thirty years of the Board of Foreign Missions of the Presbyterian Church in the United States of America.

Referring to Dr. Ashbel Green's History of Presbyterian Missions, 1741 to 1838, page viii., where a second volume of the History is adverted to, these Memoirs do not take its place. For a complete history, an immense number of letters on file in the Mission House would require examination. The plan of this book implies, however, a full acquaintance with the proceedings of the Executive Committee, to be referred to so far as may be expedient. The cause of missions was greatly favored in having such eminent clergymen as Drs. Phillips, Janeway, McElroy, Spring, and others, and such laymen of influence as Messrs. James Lenox, Walter Lowrie, David W. C. Olyphant, and others, as members of the Executive Committee. Their meetings were held every Monday morning, excepting in the month of August. They enjoyed the confidence of the church, and their councils were prospered from on high.

The editor of these Memoirs may refer to the privilege of his being connected with his revered father for many years in the same work. This resulted from separate appointments by the Board, which were not sought for by either, and at first were declined by both; but which eventually led to their occupying adjoining offices in the Mission House. Previously they had been separated, when one of them went as a missionary to India, in 1833, neither he nor his wife expecting to return to this country. In a few weeks after arriving at Calcutta she was called to her heavenly home—an event full of distress to the survivor, though of joy to herself. Their esteemed colleagues, after some months, embarked for this country, under medical orders for Mr. Reed's health; but he departed this life soon on the voyage. His classmate and colleague endeavored to fulfill their mission by going alone to the selected station, at Lodiana; but eventually had to return home for his health. Partially regaining health, he applied to the Board to be sent again to his field. Under medical counsel, this request had to be refused. Service as a pastor was then available; but by the Board it was considered that the time spent in India would be of use in the Mission House, where additional service was already required. He was thus again connected with his beloved father; and for thirty years it was his great privilege to be associated with him in his work for our blessed Lord. For nearly as long a period he has survived him, still engaged in the same work. Of late, much of his time has been occupied with these Memoirs. Imperfect as they are, may they be accepted of God, and be useful to His people!

JOHN C. LOWRIE.

53 Fifth Avenue, New York, 1895.

SUMMARY

	PAGE
A Personal Narrative, 1784–1810, . .	1
Public or Civic Life, 1811–1836, .	20
Family Life, 1806–1868, . .	28
Treatise on Divine Revelation, 1830, .	32
Foreign Missionary Subjects, .	82
Missions Among the Indians . .	134
Memorials, ...	173
Index, .	191

MEMOIRS OF WALTER LOWRIE.

A PERSONAL NARRATIVE.

I was born in the City of Edinburgh, on the 10th day of December, 1784, of poor, respectable and pious parents. My father's ancestors for several generations were of that rigid class, the Covenanters; but disliking their censorious spirit, he left them, and joined the Presbyterian Church. In it he has been a member from early age, and for many years a ruling elder. He is a man of strong and independent mind, and, though only a common English scholar, during a long life he has acquired a great deal of useful information. In every place where he has resided, he has been respected and esteemed, and has sustained the character of an honest and religious man.

My mother was from the Highlands, and belonged to the clan of the Camerons. Her Celtic ancestors for hundreds of years had lived and died amidst the heather, and the straths, and the blue, misty lakes of their own rugged country. Her father took an active part under Lochiel, the chieftain of the clan, in the rebellion of 1745, and, although he escaped with his life, he lost all his property. My parents were married young—my father in his 22d year, and my mother in her 16th year. At that time my mother could not speak a word of English, but my father, though a resident of the Lowlands, spoke the Gaelic fluently. I scarcely know an excellence of the female character which my mother does not possess. Kind, affectionate and benevolent, with deep and uniform piety, the study of her life has been to make her husband and her children happy. My father is warm in his temper, and sometimes passionate. My mother is mildness itself, and judgment, prudence and discretion mark her every step.

In August, 1792, my father, with his family, emigrated to the United States. The family consisted of a brother and three sisters older than myself, and a brother and sister younger. Two other sisters were afterwards added to the family. After a prosperous voyage, we landed in New York in September. Here my father left the family, and proceeded on foot to Huntingdon County, Penn., where one of his early friends resided, and where he purchased a small farm. The same autumn he returned to New York, and removed the family to that place. This long journey was to be made in wagons. A light wagon, with two horses, was purchased, and a wagon with four horses was hired, and in these the family proceeded slowly on their way. At Harrisburg, enn., a heavy fall of snow delayed the travellers for some days, and at Clark's Ferry, on the Susquehanna, the owner of the hired wagon refused to proceed further. The most necessary articles of baggage were put into the light wagon, and my brother and three elder sisters had to walk the remainder of the journey, over 100 miles. Previous to this time, my mother had taught me to read, and for three succeeding winters I was sent to school—the whole not exceeding ten months. With these opportunities, I learned writing, spelling, arithmetic, and some knowledge of bookkeeping. The business of farming was new to my father, and my brother, seven years older than myself, was a total stranger to every kind of labor. My father's funds were all expended on the journey and in the purchase of the farm, which was but partially improved, and much of it stony and difficult of cultivation. Under these disadvantages, for several years, many were the difficulties incident to our situation.

In my thirteenth year I was strong and large for my age, and the work of the farm was no trouble to me. The next year I was a young man, in appearance at least, and able to "make a hand," as it was called, in the harvest-field, and, indeed, in most of the work of the farm. During eight years that we remained in Huntingdon County, my opportunities of improvement were very limited. My father had a few books, all of which I read with care, and some of them twice over. Among them was perhaps the first edition of Morse's Geography, in two large volumes, 8vo. With this I was greatly delighted, and spent many a long winter evening in its careful perusal. With the historical books of the Bible I was well acquainted, but I had very little taste for the New Testament Scriptures.

In my fifteenth year I took up a book in a neigh-

bour's house, merely to see what it was. The first
words I read, were :

"All night the dreadless angel, unperceived,
 Through heaven's wide champlain held his way till morn."

I was literally charmed with the work, and forgot
that I had only come on an errand, till the owner
kindly told me to take it home. This inimitable
poem of Milton's was perused and reperused till I
could recite large portions of it from memory. The
same summer I first saw the "Pilgrim's Progress"
and the "Holy War," which also greatly delighted
me. Again and again since that time have I read all
these invaluable and original works.

In the year 1798 my father went to the western
part of the State to view the country. Next year he
sold his small farm in Huntingdon county, and made
a purchase near the Alleghany River, in the northeast corner of Butler county. I pass over various
hardships, experienced in removing his large family
and making a settlement with his limited means in a
new country. Several journeys had to be made a distance of about two hundred miles, and across the
Alleghany Mountains, in order that the cabin on the
new farm might be enlarged, the summer crop raised,
and the fall grain sowed. In the last of these journeys,
my parents and youngest sister, then an infant, were on
horseback, and I was on foot, with the care of fifteen
sheep and twenty-four hogs. The slow progress we
made induced me, when half the journey was made,
to insist that they should go on without me, and I
would follow as the flock could stand the travel.
With much reluctance they complied, and on the 9th

of December, after crossing the Laurel Hill, they left me. My difficulties commenced next day, in crossing Blacklock, a branch of the Conemaugh, on which there was neither bridge nor ferry-boat. I was obliged to wade the stream three times before I could get the flock over. This small river was twenty-five or thirty yards wide, and between two and three feet deep. The weather was excessively cold; in a few minutes my wet clothes were frozen, and it was two hours before I could reach a house of entertainment. On the evening of the 12th I reached a tavern, five miles from the Alleghany river. Early the next day a severe fall of snow commenced, accompanied with high and cold wind. With all the exercise necessary to keep the flock together, I could with difficulty keep myself warm, and it seemed sometimes that I must perish before reaching the river. When I came there, nothing could be seen but the snow, driven in every direction by the wind. The ferry-boat was on the other side of the river, and, to my repeated calls, an answer was at last returned, that, until the storm ceased, they would not venture to cross the river. I was now cold and much wearied; the nearest house was five miles distant, and, in my chilled and exhausted condition, it was impossible in such a storm to travel back those long and weary miles. The snow was now twelve inches deep, much drifted in places, and still increasing. The flock was abandoned to itself, for death now seemed to look me in the face. In this cheerless state I determined to make one more effort to warm myself, by running on the bank. Whilst thus engaged, during a slight lull in the storm, I discovered a small cabin a short distance from me on the opposite side of a ravine, where I found an Irish family sitting beside a good fire. Their hospitality was extended to me with a cordial welcome, and the best refreshments of their frugal board were set before me. Having obtained this asylum for myself, my poor flock was next to be cared for. My host went with me, and with some difficulty we placed it in a small field, the only one he had. In the evening the snow ceased falling, but the river was so full of broken ice, that to cross was impossible. In the meantime my parents had reached home, thirty miles distant, but the storm had filled them with great anxiety on my account. My brother was sent to meet me, and came to the west side of the river, while I was detained on the east. Two days afterwards, with much difficulty and danger, we got the whole flock over in canoes. My kind host was fully compensated, and with many thanks. I felt, indeed, greatly indebted to him, and long afterwards it was in my power to show his surviving partner that I had not forgotten their kindness, by aiding in procuring for her a pension, after the death of her husband, while serving as a volunteer in the War of 1812.

For the next three years, few incidents occurred worth relating. My brother, having received a severe injury from the falling of a tree, which unfitted him for the time for labor, went to New York, and for some time taught school there and in New Jersey. The labor of opening and clearing the farm, and of carrying it on, then devolved almost entirely upon me. Work, to me, was no trouble. My days were cheerful, and my sleep sound at night. My father was an industrious, careful man; all his expenditures were on the principles of strict economy. The fields were productive, and the hand of diligence brought plenty and abundance around his peaceful dwelling.

In the summer of 1802 we built a sawmill, and in the winter I sawed lumber to the amount of one hundred dollars, but did not get the raft to Pittsburg, 60 miles distant, the only market, until the next Fall.

For nearly three years there was no preaching in our neighborhood, nor indeed between Pittsburg and Erie, about 120 miles, except on a few missionary tours, in parts of this region, by ministers from the older parts of the country. In 1802 the Rev. Wm. Morehead, licentiate preacher of the Presbytery of Redstone, spent the summer in this destitute country, preaching three or four times a week in private houses, or barns, or in the open air, in places ten or fifteen miles distant from each other. In our neighbourhood, and indeed wherever he went, his preaching made a decided impression. He died December, 1802. In this and the next year, twelve Presbyterian preachers, mostly licentiates, and mostly young men, were settled in the northwestern counties of Pennsylvania, and a few of the adjoining counties of Ohio. Most of them had studied divinity with the Rev. John McMillen, D. D., of Cannonsburg, Penna. They were zealous, earnest, and, most of them, popular preachers; their coming was a great blessing to this large and destitute field of work.

In 1803 various rumors and reports reached us of revivals of religion in Kentucky and other places, accompanied with most extraordinary bodily exercises.

This work was brought to our neighbourhood in the summer, when I saw it for the first time. The subject was a young woman, an acquaintance of one of my sisters, to whose home I had come on a visit the day before. On seeing it I was very much surprised, but perfectly at a loss to account for such involuntary agitation. It continued during the whole of the sermon. Nor was I inattentive to the words of the preacher, the Rev. Robert Lea. He spoke with great earnestness and solemnity, and every word seemed to reach my heart. There was left a deep impression that I was indeed a sinner in the sight of God. We had regular preaching at home every alternate Sabbath, and every sermon deepened my distress of mind. Every evening, after service, our pastor, the Rev. Robert Johnston, had a prayer-meeting at his own house. At one of these meetings the exercises of my mind became extremely painful and distressing. Soon after the service had commenced I was struck with this extraordinary influence, as were several others about the same time. To convey a correct idea of this sensation to others is perhaps impossible. In an instant I felt that the will had no power or control over the muscles of the body. I fell backwards and suffered violent agitations, particularly of the arms, the muscles of the breast, and upper part of the body. There was no sickness, no pain, and the faculties of the mind were not the least obscured ; if any change was felt, it seemed to be in an acuteness of perception, more than usual, as to everything around me. Two of my neighbours immediately raised me, and supported me between them during the evening. When the service was ended, the influence left me,

and I walked home with several others, but preferred
to be silent rather than to converse with them. For
about six weeks the exercises of my mind were painful and often distressing. I then obtained, or thought
I obtained, "peace with God through our Lord Jesus
Christ." I know not that further details would promote any good purpose. It may be very satisfactory
for a Christian to be able to say: "At such a time
and place I was born again."

I do not doubt but there are such cases. I do not
now set so much value on such an ability as I did
formerly; nor do I know that any Christian was ever
able to derive much consolation from this kind of
knowledge. It is a far clearer point to me, that the
follower of Christ Jesus will derive more true comfort
from a constant discharge of his duty towards God,
and towards man, in the exercises of faith, and under
the influence of deep humility, with watchfulness and
prayer, than he will derive by looking back to the
state of his feelings at the time of his supposed
consecration to Christ. It is the duty of the Christian
to have his evidences always bright, and when they
become otherwise, to seek again the highway from
which he has departed. For the soul to take comfort
when in a cold and lifeless state, from its former
experience, is a comfort not free from danger, and
not, at least very clearly, indicated in the word of
God. Had David quieted his fears, after the murder
of Uriah, by referring to his former experience, had
he even taken comfort to himself, from the near and
intimate communion with God, he had often experienced, we are warranted in saying he would have
shown far less evidence of true religion, than does the

spirit which breathes in every line of the fifty-first psalm.

About the time I obtained a hope of an interest in the Saviour, the mysterious influence, which caused the bodily agitation, left me. Nor was I ever subject to it again. In the Fall of the same year I made a profession of religion, and it has been my sincere desire to live agreeably to that profession; but, alas! how unfruitful has my life so far been in the eyes of a pure and holy God! how often have I departed from the way of holiness! But by His grace I remain unto this day, and His grace is still able to sustain me to the close of life, and give me an abundant entrance to the inheritance of the saints in light.

I may add here a few lines in reference to the strange bodily exercise which at that period was so very general. My knowledge in regard to it, in our own church, and in those adjacent, was minute and exhaustive. Being myself a subject of it, there was no reserve in conversing with others under the same influence. Much was said and written on both sides of the question, some contending that it was the work of God, and others that it was the work of the devil; the first were too sanguine in their expectations of good in the results which were to follow; the last made a great mistake by condemning the whole work in advance without waiting to try it by its fruits. Among all the individuals with whom I conversed, not one was found, that in a greater or less degree, had not a personal conviction of sin. If this fact be admitted, it will follow, that up to this point, it was a work of the Spirit of God. With many, however, the conviction was very slight, and continued but a short time. Some, whose convictions were deep and distressing, were freed also from their distress, and returning to their former careless course, gave sad evidence, by their increased love of worldly pleasure, how little advantage they had derived from their previous exercises of mind. A few became in a short time more openly profane than at any former period of their lives. But others, consisting of a large number, from the age of twelve up to seventy years, by a Christian walk and conversation, have given evidence of true piety. There is no doubt that, in the excitement which influenced so many minds at once, there were many false hopes and expectations, founded on anything but the sure word of unerring truth. These are perhaps attendant more or less on every general revival of religion. When the wheat is sown, then cometh the enemy and soweth tares. Speaking of the work as a whole, I have no difficulty in calling it a revival of religion, and such a one as every Christian should rejoice to see, although attended with circumstances which induced many who did not, and who would not, examine it, to preach and to pray against it.

Soon after my mind was relieved from the distress and pressure under which I labored, I felt a strong desire to study for the ministry. For some time this feeling was confined to myself, but, being able to think of nothing else, I made known the state of my mind to my father. He did not discourage me, but pointed out the difficulties which lay in the way of my education. He had it not in his power to assist me ; on the contrary, he needed my assistance at home. Deep and anxious were my reflections on this subject, but the way was dark, and difficulties, apparently insurmountable, presented themselves on every side. In the month of December the river rose, and I took the boards, previously sawed, to Pittsburg. I found a ready market, and, in the manufacture and sale of this article, I saw the possibility of procuring means to prosecute my studies, and I returned home with the settled determination, of devoting my whole attention to that one object. In the first place, I saw that it was necessary to assist in making such arrangements for my father as would make his family comfortable ; and it was determined to build a grist mill. My brother had previously returned from New Jersey, and, with some assistance from a millwright, he undertook that part of the work. Building the mill-house, farming, and preparing more boards for market, was the work assigned to me for the year. All my exertions for that period were intended chiefly for the benefit of my father ; he had given me 150 acres for a farm, poor indeed, and unimproved, but I expected it would sell for something, and with other means assist me in the pursuit of knowledge. The summer of 1804 was passing away, and in August it became evident that the grist mill could not be finished before the new year. This was a discouraging consideration, as I was extremely anxious to commence the Latin grammar in October. In the beginning of September I was attacked with a severe sickness.

Returning home on foot, night overtook me when I had four miles to travel. The road, which was only a path, lay through a forest, and the night being quite dark, I soon lost it. After seeking in vain to find the path, I lay down at the root of a tree, and, being weary, soon fell asleep. A slight rain fell during the night, and at daylight I found myself faint and cold, and pained with a lightness in my head, never before experienced. I got home early, and assisted in bringing in the last of our harvest. In the afternoon I was attacked with an intermittent fever, so violent that in three days there was no hope of my recovery. On the fifth day I was too weak to speak, though quite sensible to everything around me. On the evening of the sixth day, about midnight, I believed I was dying, and for an hour I could not tell whether the pains of death were not already passed. This was the crisis of the disease. About two o'clock I fell asleep, and in the morning was evidently better. During the first two days I felt much peace of mind, although the sickness was known to be very serious. But when hope was given up, I had many serious conflicts. My father conversed freely with me, and suggested many precious thoughts, which gave me strength and comfort. Still, I felt that it was indeed a solemn thing to die. After the favorable crisis, my health and strength gradually returned. My sickness had much delayed the work we had on hand; it was now October, and much remained to be done. My father thought he could succeed without further assistance from me, and that it was now proper for me to turn my attention to my own pursuits. On the 8th of October, 1804, with the blessing of both my parents, I left their peaceful abode; the tears of my beloved mother flowed in abundance, while she prayed that the peace of the living God might rest upon me. For more than a year I had longed for the time when I could commence the rudiments of an education, but now, when that time had arrived, I felt a pain and reluctance in leaving my parents which I had not anticipated. The prospect before me was well calculated to induce discouragement. Near the age of twenty years, I was about to begin a long course of study without one dollar, and without the means of procuring any, except by the hard and laborious process of sawing boards, and taking them one hundred miles, by the river, to market. It was uncertain whether, without my assistance, my father could finish his mill; and, without it, the family could not subsist in comfort.

With these feelings, I commenced the study of the Latin Grammar with the Rev. Robert Johnston, who resided six miles from my father's. Two young men, my neighbors, Mr. Redick, and Mr. Crawford, had commenced with him a month before, and, by intense application, I was soon placed in the same class with them.

I remained four weeks with Mr. Johnston, and during that time my health and strength were perfectly restored. Every Saturday I returned home and stayed till Monday. On viewing the situation of my father, I was convinced that it was my duty to return home, and assist in placing him in more comfortable circumstances. During the winter we finished the mill, and in the spring, I took $100 worth of lumber to market. The most of the sum was expended in necessaries for the family, a small part of it in clothing and books for myself. On the 1st of May, I again returned to Mr. Johnston, where Messrs. Redick and Crawford still remained. They were now far before me, but I hoped to overtake them before winter. Their circumstances, however, enabled them to go to an excellent academy in Beaver County, and I was soon left to pursue my studies alone. The ministerial labors of two congregations, twelve miles apart, necessarily obliged Mr. Johnston to be much from home. My situation for improvement, therefore, was not very favorable. In these circumstances it seemed best that I should, if possible, go to the Rev. John McPherrin who was a finished scholar, and already had much experience in teaching the classics in Westmoreland County, where he formerly resided. In July I went to see him, and made known my situation and wishes to him without reserve or concealment. My situation interested him, and he expressed his willingness to take charge of my education. It was necessary, however, that I should build a cabin, in which I could have my books and my bed, as his family was large, and his house too small for themselves. It was now the 1st of August, and before I could take up my books, I had my cabin to build, and by some means liquidate my account with Mr. Johnston, and also provide some clothing for the winter. I, therefore, returned home and wrought thirty days for a neighbour at fifty cents a day, and then cut as many saw logs as, when sawed and taken to market, would pay my boarding, and expenses for the next winter. In October I built a neat cabin of logs, twelve feet square, with a chimney in one end, built of cat and clay. This was finished early in November, and I returned home, seventeen miles distant, to assist my father in building a fire-house over the water-wheel of the mill. It was with great reluctance he received my assistance as the time was past when I expected to have been at my books, but the necessity of the measure was urgent because, without it, the mill would have

been impeded by the frost for the greater part of the
winter.   On the 19th of November, 1805, we had the
house completed, and next day I once more bade adieu
to my parents, and early the same day reached Mr.
McPherrin's, where I was cordially received.

I had now resumed my studies, with better hopes
and prospects than at any time heretofore, and the
most unremitting attention and diligence were be-
stowed upon my books.   I went to bed between ten
and eleven, and always rose at four in the morning.
At five Mr. McPherrin came to hear me recite.   In
the winter this was long before day, but he was
always in the habit of rising at five o'clock.   Excepting at breakfast and family prayers, I was not seen
out of my study-house until dinner-time, about one
o'clock.   I then, for two hours, assisted the boys in
their work, of which providing firewood was the
principal part.   I had then the evening undisturbed
until ten o'clock.   In a large log house, such as the
family occupied, it was necessary in the winter to
keep a large fire burning day and night, and hence
the consumption of fuel was very great.   Every
Saturday afternoon I assisted them in hauling from
the fields a stock for the ensuing week.   In working
in wood I had acquired a good degree of skill, and I
could do many things that would have required a
carpenter.   I was scarcely a moment unemployed,
and was glad to be useful, and performed these services most cheerfully; and as the farm was unimproved, and the barn and outbuildings were out of
order, many repairs were needed.   Out of doors Mr.
McPherrin was often with me, and treated me with
the utmost kindness and regard.   Many clergymen in
passing staid a night with us, and generally shared

a part of my bed. One of these mentioned my preceptor's warm satisfaction with my progress in study. By this time I was fully satisfied that with diligence and perseverance I could master these three languages —the Latin, Greek and Hebrew—without further instruction. The months of April and May, 1807, found me again engaged at the sawmill. This I intended to be the last work of the kind, because the labor was so severe, I feared its effects on my constitution. The proceeds, after paying all my debts, left me forty dollars, which I gave to my father. On my return through Butler, I made arrangements to take up an English school there. On the 17th of June, 1807, I took leave of Mr. McPherrin and his amiable family, and, without money, with only a few books and a few clothes, took up my residence in Butler, intending to sojourn there for a year.

My school consisted of forty scholars, all learning the common branches of an English education. The tuition was six dollars per annum each, while my boarding and washing cost me one hundred dollars. I had, however, nearly the half of the day to myself, and I found the teaching to be more like recreation than labour. I soon got the good will of my pupils. They were of both sexes, and some of them were young men and young women. I became much interested in them, and their parents were quite satisfied with their improvement. I found no difficulty, and indeed not much hindrance in the study of Latin and Greek, but for want of Hebrew books no progress was then made in that language. In October, unsolicited, I received the appointment of Clerk to the County Commissioners, at a salary of eighty dollars a year, these officers kindly permitting me to be

absent during school hours on condition that I would
bring up the business in the evening.

The preceding autobiographical narrative was
written in the winter of 1824-25. With omissions, it
is now printed, as giving information concerning the
life and character treated of in this volume.

The school in Butler did not imply that the call to
the ministry had been laid aside. It was as yet in
its earlier stages, a strong desire, a purpose, if it were
the will of the Lord; but not as yet so far settled as
to be brought to the consideration of the Presbytery
—according to the usual rule. Providential circumstances led to some delay.

Afterwards it became evident that other lines of
duty required attention, leading to public service as
a layman, and later still to his long life-work—as
hereinafter related.

Several months after taking charge of the school,
January 14, 1808, he was married to Miss Amelia
McPherrin, daughter of the Rev. John and Mrs. Mary
McPherrin, of Butler County, Penna.

In 1808 Mr. and Mrs. Lowrie made their home in
Butler, the chief town of Butler County, Penna. It
was then a small but pleasant village of a few hundred inhabitants; now it is one of the important
towns of the State. Besides his school and the Commissioners' clerkship, opportunities of surveying
lands, and of aiding to settle land titles and claims, were
available—at first in a limited degree—the country
was newly inhabited. Proprietors of large sections
of land lived in the eastern parts of the State; new
settlers, as farmers and as tenants, were coming into

the western counties ; a thorough knowledge of "land questions," coupled with growing reputation for integrity, ability, energy and sympathy, were good conditions of success in business life. The sterling character of his venerable father, a farmer and mill-owner, and an honoured elder in the Presbyterian Church, contributed not a little to his son's being welcomed in his plans of self-support. To these good conditions may well be added the lovely character and grace of his wife, known to many as the daughter of an admirable mother and of the most eminent clergyman in the county. Referring to public life, it was no doubt the growing acquaintance of the young teacher with the farming people and their interests in the northwestern counties, that led largely to his election in 1811 as a member of the Pennsylvania Legislature—in the House of Representatives one year, and in the Senate six years. In 1818, while still in the Senate, he was elected as a member of the United States Senate, full term.

IT is the plan of this book to give but brief accounts of public or civic affairs in which Mr. Lowrie was now engaged. These are accessible in the Journals or Minutes of the two Legislatures and in the newspaper reports of their proceedings. General interest in most of those subjects has long since passed away. Yet the earlier years of the century, now near its end, were largely the formative period of the great central west of our country, extending from the Alleghany Mountains in Pennsylvania westward. It was of the greatest importance that both the State and the National councils should contain members well acquainted with all matters of public interest. And many of them were such men in a high degree.

In Western Pennsylvania, with special enactments of the Legislature cordially granted, the subjects of Land Titles and Taxation, Public Roads, Navigation of Rivers, Common Schools, Colleges, etc., received almost special favour from the State. Among other things, an unusual Commission was organized, consisting of a State member from each of five States : Pennsylvania, Virginia, Ohio, Kentucky and Indiana, of which Mr. Lowrie was chairman. The Commission employed a sufficient number of qualified agents and labourers, to survey the Ohio river, from Pittsburgh to Louisville, some 700 miles ; and to remove obstacles to its better navigation, so far as practicable. Each of these States was in a more or less degree favorable to this object, owing to its own borders on this river. It was a measure that required skillful and difficult labour and much fatigue, for several months, and considerable expense ; but it was one of far-seeing wisdom and great benefit—not only to the five States, but to other large sections of the country, west, northwest and southwest.

Later "improvements" have, no doubt, since been made ; but these showed a wise energy and forecast for that early day. And to the Ohio, or "Beautiful River," as the Indians called it, may now be added the great commercial value of its chief affluents, the Alleghany and the Monongahela, besides its lesser tributaries. Few systems of river navigation combine usefulness and beauty to so great a degree.

FROM A STATE TO THE NATIONAL SENATE.

In the change from Harrisburg to Washington, Mr. Lowrie found his duties similar in some respects, but quite different in others. In the former, the State and its local interests chiefly occupied his attention ; in the latter, broader, more varied, national and foreign, as well as home, matters required careful study. The members of the National Senate, moreover, had been brought up in different parts of the country, and in differing family and social circumstances ; but in cases not a few the home training, education, social and religious life of the senators had been very similar. They were all proud of their national history, and full of hope as to the future. They were Americans, all. It was no doubt an advantage to the member from Pennsylvania that he had been a member of its Senate. Much depends on practical experience in the dispatch of legislative business. The business itself, its bearings, progress and results need to be well considered in the light of general principles and previous knowledge. Of course, fairness, courtesy, kindness—in brief, the observance of the Golden Rule—should mark the personal intercourse of the members of a legislative assembly, and greatly influence their public action.

At Washington many subjects required the consideration of the Upper House. Some of them were matters of routine, such as the confirmation of appointments to public office ; even these were often of great moment. Some of these subjects were peculiar to our country, such as the organization of Territories on the frontier, and the admission of new States to the Union. Others were the national finances, public lands, Indian affairs, foreign commerce, and many more. In 1819–23 slavery or anti-slavery in the Territories became a very urgent subject, growing out of the application of settlers in the Territory of Missouri to be received into the Union as a slaveholding State. Most, if not all, of the Southern States contended for the right of holding slaves in a Territory, and as a State. This was strongly opposed by the Northern States. The discussion of the subject in both Houses of Congress was long, earnest, and at times ominous of "the breaking up of the Union." In these discussions, as a member representing one of the central border States, and having clear convictions of what was right in itself, as well as best for the country, Mr. Lowrie could not but take a decided part—adverse to the extension of slaveholding. But, known as a man of firm, yet not aggressive nor partisan, views, and being on good terms socially with his fellow members, his influence would be recognized as not unfriendly, while yet as sure to be exerted in favour of liberty. The so-called "Missouri Compromise" ended the discussions of 1820. He had actively supported what he conscientiously considered the right side of the subject; and he closed one of his speeches, after expressing deep regret at the troubled outlook as to the dissolution of the Union by saying: "If the alternative be this: either dissolution of the Union, or the extension of slavery over this whole western country, I for one will choose the former."

On Standing Committees it is interesting to note that of the Committee of Finance, evidently one of the most important, Mr. Lowrie was a member for six years; on Public Lands, six years; on Indian Affairs, one year; besides others. A reader of the Senate's proceedings, in the official and newspaper reports, would seldom find that he made long speeches, though in some instances they were quite extended, and always worthy of their subjects. Brief remarks by him were common, attractive, always appropriate. Evidently he gave close attention to the business in hand, and as a rule he was always in his place. He was on kind terms with all, so far as was known, and was on intimate terms of friendship with several members—some of them those best known to the country, including several from southern and western States. His own judgment was that the Senate included in its membership many of the best men, as to character, ability, and all qualifications needful to secure the highest confidence of their neighbours at home and their countrymen at large.

One of his constituents in Pennsylvania wrote to him, about this time, asking the favour of his recommendation to the President for an appointment to some office. Most members of Congress are burdened with requests of this same kind. On mentioning the case, without urging it, the President, in reply, read to him a letter which he had received from a distinguished general, counselling him to adopt the policy of making official appointments from both the leading political parties of the country. Eventually this counsel became known to the public, and was criticised after the general had become a candidate for a high office. The President was then inquired of in regard to the letter; but he had no recollection of it —virtually a denial of having received such a letter. The general did not remember having written it. He was not then in public life, and might easily have forgotten it. The subject was taken up by the party newspapers. The senator was violently criticised for reporting that such a letter had been received, when the President knew nothing of it; and although he had taken little interest in the case, his name was not the less denounced.

But it had so happened that the President had read the same letter to at least two of the senators, both from Pennsylvania—one of them, Mr. Lacock, the other, Mr. Roberts, both of them gentlemen of the highest character and standing. All three concurred in their statements of the facts of the case— the two ex-senators unqualifiedly; and also that nothing whatever was said by the President of any letter as being intended for private use. These statements were made public at that time.

This case was doubtless well understood by the members of the U. S. Senate; and most of them, probably all of them, were aware that Mr. Lowrie would not return to Washington as a senator; and also that he was not a candidate for any office. The office of secretary of the Senate, then almost an office for life, was soon to become vacant. It was then an office which required its incumbent to possess qualifications in most respects similar to those of the senators themselves, and to be efficient and trustworthy in the highest degree. To this office he was elected by a large vote of the Senate, December 25, 1825. This office was accepted, and its duties immediately entered upon. It was not an office that involved frequent and painful separations from his family. Washington City became chiefly their home; though they spent their summer months at their former residence in Butler.

COLONIZATION SOCIETY—CHINESE LANGUAGE.

While in Washington Mr. Lowrie became a member of the Executive Committee of the American Colonization Society; which he favoured with his pen, his counsels and other services. A weekly meeting for prayer was held at his house during sessions of Congress, which was welcomed by some of the members of different religious denominations, and regarded with real interest. There also a Congressional Temperance Society was organized.

His linguistic talents were somewhat remarkable. The Latin, Greek and Hebrew languages were probably better known by him than by many clergymen. When about forty years of age, he took up the Chinese language, in addition to his previous engagements; and in a few years he had made such progress in this peculiar language, as to make translations of the simpler Chinese works. The knowledge thus acquired was, of course, imperfect, but it became practically important afterwards, as enabling him to appreciate the method of printing Chinese books on divisible metallic types, instead of the carved solid wooden blocks, engraved. The remarkably conservative Chinese do not yet generally adopt this new and great invention, adhering to their old customs; but the new method is in practical use on a large scale. It is already employed largely in printing stereotype editions of the Holy Scriptures and other books in Chinese. Further particulars may be found in Dr. Green's Presbyterian Missions, page 178.

CARE FOR AGED PARENTS.

In the town of Butler, an elder brother of Mr. Lowrie, a prominent citizen of Pittsburgh, united with him in opening a store for miscellaneous goods, providing the capital for it, and engaging for its management a well-qualified agent. It was kept up for some years with satisfactory success, and then disposed of without loss—neither of the proprietors having sufficient time at command to meet its requirements.

One of their objects was to make a home for their now aged parents, whose large family of sons and daughters had all been married and settled in homes of their own, hardly any of them near the old homestead. For the venerable parents a pleasant cottage had been built by the younger brother on his own ground in the village, not far from the store; and occupation was given to his still vigorous mind by having a certain charge of its business. The editor of this memoir, then a student in the Academy, was also assigned to the store for a few hours daily, chiefly as 'company' for his revered grandfather.

It was probably of much greater benefi to the grand-son than to his aged relative, whose wise and kind counsels were invaluable; though the opportunity of gaining some knowledge of business matters was prized. At first the grandparents were delighted with these arrangements; but after trial of village life, they became weary of it, and longed for a home again in the country. Their sons then obtained for them an excellent home in the family of a widowed daughter, their beloved sister, where the aged parents spent their remaining years in comfort, enjoying the blessedness of the righteous. He died at the age of ninety-three; his wife, a few years earlier. He was a thoroughly good and upright man, and was held in great regard by all who knew him. His wife was always a benediction to him and to their children and grandchildren. She was lovely and greatly beloved.

FAMILY LIFE.

DECLINING RE-ELECTION AS A SENATOR.

For eighteen years the absence of Mr. Lowrie from his home and family in the winter months had been the trial of their life. In those days a two weeks' journey, on horseback each way, was required for a visit to his family in the holidays, involving too long an absence from official duty, besides expense and fatigue. The latter were but minor matters compared with the claims of his wife and children. No man was ever more attached to his family and home. His wife had given a very reluctant consent to these winter separations, and with health becoming delicate, and a growing family, mostly of boys, it seemed evident that an entire change must be made. His declining to be a candidate for re-election was the decision. He could otherwise be well employed, without being so much separated from his beloved family. The path of duty seemed to be plain. His intended withdrawal from public service became known, in 1824, to his friends, and was a matter all settled.

DEATH OF MRS. LOWRIE.

In 1832, November 5th, after twenty-four years of married life, Mr. Lowrie met with his greatest sorrow and loss—the death of his wife. She was the mother of their eight children ; a woman greatly beloved in

her own family, and by a large number of relatives
and neighbors. She died at Bedford, Penna., on her
journey to Washington with her husband and
younger children; but her funeral and interment were
from her home in Butler the following winter, attended by all the people of the town, the rich and
poor alike. Lovely and loving, genial, discreet, devoted to our Saviour and His service, abounding in
works of charity, visiting the poorest with her sympa-
thizing ministry and her prayers; in the midst of the
usually allotted years of life, in the centre of her own
loving home, she yet had "a desire to depart and to
be with Christ, for it is very far better." This
bereavement was followed in a few months by her
eldest son and his wife leaving for India as missionaries, towards which her sympathies and her prayers
had no doubt great influence, though she was not
spared to see them embark.

At the farewell religious services in the Arch
Street Church, Philadelphia, in the following May,
as quoted from a periodical of that city, in
June, 1833, her husband, the Hon. Walter Lowrie,
who was present at the meeting, was urged by friends
to say a few words. "He then referred to the attach-
ment which a father might be supposed to feel toward a dutiful and affectionate son, an eldest son, and
especially toward a son whose piety and self-consecra-
tion to the missionary work were associated with the
counsels and prayers of the departed wife, the sainted
mother, whose eminent Christian graces and attainments the occasion seemed so forcibly to recall. But
he assured his Christian friends that, though he felt,
and felt deeply, at parting with these children, yet,
instead of any reluctancy or regret, he could say that

he was willing, and even anxious, that they should
go ; that if there was any station which he envied, it
was that which they were about to assume ; and that
he could freely part with every child he had if they
were called to leave their native shores on such an
errand. . . ."

"But to give a just summary of these remarks, or
an idea of the manner in which they were stated, the
effect which they produced upon those who heard
them, were utterly impossible. It is sufficient to say
of the meeting, taken as a whole, that the God of
Missions appeared to have made it a season of unusual
and precious enjoyment to many of His people, and
one whose whole effect on the cause of missions in
future time will not be lost."

The family of Mr. and Mrs. Lowrie included eight
children—six sons and two daughters. The eldest
son, born December 16, 1808, went to India as a missionary in 1833. His wife died in Calcutta November
21, 1833, a few weeks after their arrival. The second
son was born April 13, 1811. He was a lawyer. He
died February 4, 1836. The first daughter, born
June 12, 1814, was married to a merchant of Pittsburg, and died July 1, 1887. The second daughter
was born January 12, 1816, and died September
17, 1834. The third son was born February 18,
1819, and went to China as a missionary. He was
murdered by Chinese pirates, near Ningpo, August 18,
1847. The fourth son was born March 16, 1823. He
was a lawyer, and an elder in the Presbyterian
Church. He was married. He died December 10,

1885. The fifth son was born November 24, 1827. He went to China as a missionary with his wife in 1854. He died April 26, 1860. His widow, and their son and daughter, are missionaries in China—the daughter married to a medical-missionary from New York. The youngest child, Henry Martyn, was born in Washington City, March 16, 1830, and died in Butler, June 26, 1831. Concerning all those who have departed this life, there was a blessed hope in the death of each one.

DIVINE REVELATION.

Among Mr. Lowrie's papers, under dates of May and September, 1830, has been found a somewhat extended Treatise on Divine Revelation—presumably from his pen, originally. The first part of this treatise is here inserted ; the second and larger part may be published hereafter. It may be remembered that he had begun studies for the ministry in his earlier life ; and his reading in subsequent years was founded not a little on his knowledge of the Sacred Scriptures in their languages ; but it does not appear that at any subsequent period of his life he had intended to resume his purpose of seeking admission to the sacred office.

————

1. Divine Revelation is a discovery made by God to man, of Himself, and of His will, higher and clearer than He has made known by the light of nature, or than man can discover by his unassisted reason.

2. Divine Revelation is possible. No man, with the use of his reason, can deny the being of a God. A wicked man may wish, in his heart, that there were no God ; but if atheism have an existence, it is but another name for insanity. No man can deny or disbelieve that he is himself a thinking being ;—he knows that he exists, and that he can act and think ; —to doubt the consciousness of his own existence is to establish its reality. He knows, too, that he did not make himself,—that he is indebted for his being

to Another. As little can any man disbelieve the evidence of his senses. He knows that he can see, and and hear, and feel, and taste, and smell the objects around him, according to the respective properties of those objects. But his consciousness and his senses all afford him the highest possible evidence of the existence of a supreme Being, of infinite power, wisdom and knowledge. This is one degree of revelation, made to man through his senses, and his rational faculties and powers. But if the power of God be infinite, all degrees of power are alike to Him; and the clearness, or the obscurity, of the revelation of Himself, to His creatures, must rest with Himself; whether it be with the clearness enjoyed by the angels around His throne or the obscurity of man upon earth.

II. NECESSITY OF A DIVINE REVELATION.

3. This subject is embarrassed with some considerations which do not properly belong to it. Where there was no Divine Revelation, the darkness was so great that its necessity was but dimly discovered by a few wise and reflecting men. Where Divine Revelation has been known for centuries, as among Christian nations, the light is so great, so diffused, so incorporated with all our thoughts and reflections, that many, using that very light, attempt to prove that it is not necessary. Take, for instance, the character of God, as revealed in the Bible. The sublime descriptions of the Divine Being, embracing every perfection and excellence, seem at once to be reasonable, and hence are claimed as the effort of reason, when unassisted reason never did discover, and never could have discovered those perfections.

4. With these remarks, let us look at the condition of those nations, ancient and modern, which were
without the light of Divine Revelation. Through
a long course of ages, what has unassisted reason
achieved for them?

The Egyptians, Greeks, and Romans were enlightened and civilized nations, but without Divine Revelation. There we find them grossly ignorant of the
most vital and important truths. Their gods were
multiplied almost without number. The sun, the
moon, and the stars,—demons, and departed heroes,—
animals, noxious insects, and even rivers were their
gods. Statues of gold and silver, blocks of wood and
of stone, the work of their own hands, were the objects
of their idolatry; and human sacrifices, obscenity,
prostitution, drunkenness and Bacchanalian revels
formed a great part of their stated worship.

5. They were ignorant of the true account of
creation,—of God's design in making the world,—of
the origin of evil, and the original dignity of human
nature. Socrates, Cicero, and Seneca, their wisest and
best men, doubted even the immortality of the soul.
Of the resurrection of the body, they knew nothing.
When such men were thus enshrouded in doubt, what
must have been the darkness of the mass of the common people? who on all these points had an equally
vital interest.

6. A future state of rewards and punishments was
too little understood to have a proper influence on
the conduct. Hence their morals were corrupt, and
corresponded with the moral darkness of the mind.
It could not be otherwise. Man is a creature actuated
by motives. But where was the motive for holiness,
for purity of heart and life, when holiness and the

worship of the heart was not known? It is remarkable, also, that the most civilized and the most barbarous nations were nearly alike in their ignorance of divine things, and in their moral depravity of conduct.

7. This picture of the nations of antiquity, drawn at large by their own historians, will suit the heathen nations of our own time; and here, too, moral darkness and depravity bring to a level the most civilized and the most barbarous. The Chinese, the Burman, take rank here with the American savage and the inhabitant of benighted Africa. The human sacrifices of New Zealand, the slaughter of his attendants at the death of an African king, the funeral piles of India, and the Car of Juggernaut, proclaim with dying groans the necessity of a Divine Revelation.

8. That much moral evil exists in the world is inscribed on every page of its history. At all times, and in all places, the record shows not slight imperfections only, but crimes which the light of reason strongly condemns. By the universal consent of all nations, man is chargeable with guilt; and when his conduct and his actions are arraigned, the verdict must be that of guilty. That this is the actual condition of mankind cannot be questioned. Now the very nature of guilt involves a liability to, and desert of, just punishment. How, then, can the justice of God be satisfied without the punishment of the guilty? Will He extend mercy and pardon, and remit the punishment which justice requires? Does not the infinite perfection of His nature require that the glorious attribute of justice be fully satisfied? If mercy can be exercised, is it the will of God that it should be exercised? And, if so, in what way or on

what terms? All these are questions which unassisted reason never did answer, and never could have answered. The more we try to answer them by reason, the more the darkness increases. Do we argue in favour of mercy? We arraign the justice of the punishment. Do we consider the high claims of infinite justice? Then the case of sinful men is hopeless. How are the claims of mercy and justice to be reconciled? If infinite wisdom be required to devise a way by which the claims of both are preserved—can finite, unassisted reason discover that plan? And can it also discover that God is willing to execute that plan? It is impossible—utterly impossible. Until God reveal these things, the highest created intelligences must remain ignorant of them; and, when revealed, it is no wonder that the angels should desire to look into them. If, therefore, a knowledge of everything dear to man—a knowledge of his eternal well-being, a knowledge of the true God, be necessary, then is a Divine Revelation necessary.

III. NEW TESTAMENT GENUINE AND AUTHENIC.

9. The books of the New Testament contain the history of Jesus Christ, the first propagation of His religion, and the' principles and precepts of Christianity. They are usually printed together, and bound in one volume, and by many are considered as but one book. They consist, however, of the writings of eight different authors, and of twenty-seven different books, written at different times, and in different parts of the world.

10. The writers of the New Testament claim to have been cotemporary with Him, whose birth, life, pre-

cepts, miracles, death and resurrection they record. They purport to relate what they heard and what they saw. Whatever they have written of Him, of His precepts, of His miracles, or of the spread of His kingdom, either by a direct historical record of facts, or by incidental allusion, they have written as eye and ear witnesses. "That which they had heard, which they had seen with their eyes, which they had looked upon, and their hands had handled" is claimed by them to have been recorded in the books of the New Testament.

11. These witnesses write with impartiality, sobriety, modesty, and every mark of sincerity. They relate their own mistakes, and record their own follies and their faults. There is no enthusiasm, no exclamations against others, no violence. Their testimony is consistent in all its parts. In no one instance is any of them in the least degree inconsistent with himself. With each other there is no contradiction, and the variance in minor points, of incidents and circumstances, shews they neither wrote in concert nor copied from each other. They gave the highest proof of their sincerity, in sealing their testimony by voluntary martyrdom. It is not to be conceived that such a number of witnesses would resign their means of support, fortune, character, and life itself for the assertion of what they knew to be false. They at least believed the truth of their testimony, and it only remains to be proved that, if they believed it to be true, they could not be deceived, and that it must be true indeed.

12. The testimony of these writers did not relate to opinions, nor to abstract points, nor to events distant in time or place; but to facts which they personally

witnessed. By the word of Jesus Christ, they witnessed the blind made to see, the lame to walk, the
deaf to hear, and the dead to rise from the grave.
They heard a Voice from heaven saying, "This is my
beloved Son, hear ye Him." They saw this same Jesus
nailed to the cross, they saw His side pierced
with a spear, and blood and water flowing from the
wound, and they saw Him laid in the tomb. After
three days He shewed himself openly to them, he ate
and drank in their presence, and conversed with them
for the space of forty days. He reproved their unbelief, and required them to handle Him and see that
it was indeed Himself. He called on Thomas in the
presence of the others, to put his fingers into the prints
of the nails, and to thrust his hand into His side.
Finally He led them out as far as Bethany, and in
their sight, and in open day, ascended up into heaven.
After His ascension, they themselves, in the name of
Jesus of Nazareth, healed the sick, caused the blind
to see, the deaf to hear, the lame to walk, and the
dead to arise. These are but a few of the prominent
facts recorded in their testimony; and in these facts
they could not possibly be deceived. In this aspect
of the argument, the alternative is presented that
their testimony is true, or that they sacrificed their
time, their good name, their every earthly comfort,
and finally their lives, to impose a falsehood on the
world.

13. As these witnesses were not themselves deceived, neither could they deceive others. The facts
they relate were public, done openly, before men of
learning, sagacity and power: as well as before multi
tudes of all other classes. If it were false that "the
blind and the lame came to Jesus in the temple, and

He healed them," could not His bitter and relentless enemies have shown it was a falsehood? If it were false that Lazarus, after lying four days in the grave, was restored to life, would it not have been more natural for the chief priests to have exposed the falsehood than to have taken counsel to put Him to death? In all places, and in the most public manner, the apostles bear their testimony to the truth of the fact that Jesus Christ rose from the dead and ascended up into heaven. In the Epistle to the Church at Corinth, reference is made to five hundred who had seen Him after the resurrection, most of whom were then living. The miracles which they performed, were all wrought in His name. In the face of the Jewish council, when actually beaten, and threatened with death, they openly state and adhere to this fact, and charge their very judges with His blood. The miracles they wrought in Jerusalem and in all parts of the Roman Empire, and the power they communicated to others of working miracles, were public and known to all. These miracles being recorded in the historical books, and referred to in the various epistles to the different churches, gives us, as will be hereafter fully shown, the testimony of that whole generation to the truth of the facts thus set forth.

14. The Jews were the most violent opposers and haters of Christianity at its beginning, and have continued to the present day to be its most bitter adversaries. Had the books of the New Testament been forgeries of the time they claim to have been written, or had they contained falsehoods, the Jews were both able and willing to have detected the imposture. The things recorded, as already stated, were not said to be done in a corner. The scene of many of the trans-

actions recorded, and especially of the crucifixion and resurrection of Jesus Christ, was Jerusalem, the metropolis of the nation. The highest civil and ecclesiastical rulers of the Jews are referred to by name as actors and as witnesses. The name of the Roman governor is given, and his actions in the scene, and what he said, are minutely set down. Dates are given, places are designated, officers, men and measures are all described. On the supposition of forgery or falsehood it is unaccountable that these things could have passed without exposure. Nor could these writings have been forgeries of a later period, because the Jews still continued their hatred of Christianity, ever watchful to avail themselves of anything to cast odium on that hated name.

15. The primitive Christians of Rome, Corinth, Galatia and other places would not have received those writings as genuine if they had been forgeries. In the epistles to these churches the facts recorded in the historical books are taken for granted, and referred to as known to all. The Apostle Paul writes of his previous labours amongst them, He reproves one church for departing from the right way after the miracles they had seen; he reproves another church for permitting a scandalous incest to remain uncensured; he speaks of the gift of tongues, and other gifts possessed by some of themselves; in his epistle to another church he calls over by name twenty-six of its members. Now if these epistles had been forgeries, it was impossible that these churches should have received them as the genuine writings of St. Paul. Deceived on this subject these churches could not be. They knew whether or not he had ever preached among them. The church in Galatia knew

whether or not they had seen the miracles to which he referred, and whether or not there was ground for his censures ; the church at Corinth knew whether or not a disgraceful incest had taken place ; and the church at Rome knew whether or not the twenty-six persons named by the apostle were of their community.   Yet, with all this knowledge, and many items more which might be detailed in these and other churches to which epistles were written, it is a fact that these very epistles were received by them as genuine and authentic.

16. Let it be assumed, what indeed needs no proof, that there exist at this day numerous Christian churches in the world ; that these churches have teachers, and rules, and ordinances, and stated times for public worship ; that they all profess to believe that Jesus Christ was the author of this religion ; that He appointed these ordinances and rules and directed them so to meet for public worship ; and that the books in which all these things are recorded claim to have been written by His immediate followers. These things, being assumed or proved, it follows that the present generation did not forge these writings. It is not impossible that books should have been forged in our age, but, on the supposition of such forgery, it is impossible that these books should have been received as genuine by all the Christian churches throughout the world.   If these books did not exist till the present age, how came these Christian churches into existence ?   And how came those societies to acknowledge, and venerate, and profess to be regulated by, books which did not even exist ? We do know, therefore, most certainly that the forgery, if it be a forgery, did not take place in our day.

It is as impossible, moreover, that a forgery of the kind supposed could have been imposed on the generation immediately preceding the present. They stood as we now stand, with the same means of judging, with the same ability to detect imposture or forgery. Christian churches existed also in their day, and by those churches were these writings received and venerated. Now these considerations apply with equal force to each of the sixty generations which have existed since the days of the apostles.

17. The citizens of the United States are in the habit of celebrating annually the day of the nation's birth. Whilst that celebration continues it is the annual testimony of a whole people to the truth of the fact that on the 4th day of July, 1776, the Declaration of Independence was adopted. Should any one pronounce this state paper to be a forgery of last year we would consider him insane. If we reasoned with him at all, we might ask how, on the supposition of forgery, he accounted for the existence of the United States as a free and independent people, governed by laws of their own and by agents of their own? Or should he pronounce it a forgery of 1796, the question still recurs, if it be a forgery of that or any other period, how and when did the United States become an independent nation? Would the generation of 1776 have received this document unless it had been both genuine and authentic? And that they knew the facts to which it referred to be true? To suppose the contrary is to suppose what is impossible and absurd. This familiar illustration applies with all its force to the books of the New Testament. The reasoning in the one case, with all its simplicity and clearness, applies with equal simplicity and clearness

to the other. And, as it is impossible that the Declaration of Independence could have been a forgery of 1776 or of any later period, so it is equally impossible that the Christian Scriptures could have been a forgery of the time they purport to have been written or of any later period. The era of the one is annually celebrated by the whole people of the United States; the era of the other is also statedly celebrated by the whole Christian Church in her solemn ordinances. The Declaration of Independence records the birth of an independent nation, which exists at the present day; the New Testament records the beginning of the Christian Church, which also exists at the present day. The one was received as genuine and authentic by our fathers of 1776, because they had knowledge of the truth of the facts to which it refers. In the truth of those facts they could not be deceived. They were written with the blood of fathers, husbands, sons—mothers, wives and daughters. They witnessed and endured scenes of desolation, distress and misery on every side; and in all these thousands of themselves were the sufferers. It is mockery, not reasoning, to say that in these facts they could have been deceived. And how was it with the generation of the New Testament writers? The first history of the Christian Church was also written in the blood of fathers and mothers, husbands, wives and children. They, too, endured the spoiling of their goods; they were persecuted, vilified and oppressed, and their very names cast out as evil; and, for the truth of what they saw and what they believed, they suffered death in all its forms. And will it be contended that, with the most ample means of knowing the truth, they suffered all these things for a forgery or a falsehood?

18. Let us now see what is the evidence of history on this question. Here the evidence negatively is complete. The Jewish historian, Josephus, was a cotemporary of some of the writers of the New Testament. He writes the history of the same period, and relates some things in common with them; but he never intimates that those writings were forged or false. Nor does any other Jewish writer, nor do the Roman historians of that or any later period in the least degree intimate a suspicion of forgery or falsehood. On the contrary, Josephus, in his history of Herod the Great, of Archelaus and of Pontius Pilate, by reference to dates, customs, parties, and to various other points, confirms the New Testament history; and the Roman historians, as will be shown hereafter, expressly state that the life of Jesus Christ was written by His immediate followers.

19. The direct affirmative historical evidence is full and conclusive. The books of the New Testament have been quoted and referred to by a continued series of Christian and other writers from the days of the apostles till the present time.

In the first century we have the five Christian fathers—Barnabas, Clement, Hermas, Ignatius and Polycarp. These writers were contemporaries of the apostles, and the first three are named in the New Testament. They all refer to the books of the New Testament as genuine and authentic Scriptures, received and relied on by the whole Christian Church.

20. In the second century we have the following writers,* who in like manner bear their testimony

---

* For a detailed account of the Christian and heathen writers, see Appendix, No. 1. See Lardner's *Credibility of the Gospel History,* British Encyclopædia, ninth edition.

to the writings of the New Testament: Papias, in
Necropolis, A.D. 114; Justin Martyr, Palestine, 140;
Tatian, 170; Hegerippus, 170; Ireneus, Lyon, 170;
Athenagorus, 180; Theophilus, Antioch, 181; Clement, Alexandia, 180; Tertullian, Carthage, 190.

21. In the third century, Ammonius, A.D. 220;
Julius Africanno, 220; Hippolytus, 225; Origen, 240;
Cyprian, Carthage, 250; Dionysius, Rome, 260; Commodian, 270; Theognostus, 270; Victorinus, Germany,
290; Methodius, Tyre, 290; Philias, Egypt, 296.

22. In the fourth century Eusebius, the historian,
315; Marcellus, 320; Athanasius, 326; Juvenius, Spain,
345; Council of Laodicea, 363; Basil, Cappadocia, 370;
Jerome, 372; Gregory, 375; Augustin, 394. Several
of these writers have left us a catalogue of the books
of the New Testament, agreeing with the names of the
books as we now have them. So also did the Third
Council of Carthage, A.D. 397.

23. During the first, second and third centuries,
various heresies sprung up in the bosom of the church.
The writings of those who advocated these heresies in
various ways afford evidence that the books of the New
Testament are genuine and authentic. Thus the Ebionites received the gospel by Matthew, but rejected all
the epistles of Paul, whom they called an apostate, because he departed from the Levitical law. On the
other hand, the Gnostics contended that the gospel by
Matthew, the epistle to the Hebrews, and those of
Peter and John, were writings for Jews, not for
Christians. All these contests prove the existence of
the books of the New Testament.

24. Tacitus, a Roman historian and a heathen,
states that this pernicious superstition took its rise
from Christ, who, in the reign of Tiberias Cæsar, was

put to death by Pontius Pilate ; that it spread rapidly and had infected great numbers in Rome itself ; and that the Christians suffered a dreadful persecution in Rome by order of Nero, A.D. 65.

The celebrated letters of the younger Pliny to the Emperor Trajan prove that the knowledge of Christianity was general in Pontus and Bythinia ; he states, also, the purity of the lives and the fortitude of the Christians under suffering. The persecution they then endured was the subject of the letter, A. D. 106.

Celsus, A.D. 176, mentions some of the disciples by name, and quotes many passages from the books of the New Testament. He admits most of the facts of the gospel history. He professed to draw his arguments from the writings received by the Christian church, especially the four gospels, and in no one instance from any other writings.

Porphyry, that sensible, learned, but severe and unfair, enemy of Christianity, bears a testimony equally conclusive to the authenticity of the books of the New Testament. He possessed every advantage, which learning, natural abilities or political situation could afford, but, sagacious and acute as he was, he never attempted to deny that the books of the New Testament were genuine. He wrote against the Christians A. D. 263.

One hundred years later, A. D. 360, flourished the Emperor Julian. He systematically and most insidiously set himself to root out Christianity from his empire. He names the four Gospels,—notices the difference between them, and refers to the Acts of the Apostles. In numerous instances he refers to the customs and worship of the Christian church ; and, in his attempts to reform the Pagan superstition, his arguments and his exhortations are drawn from the Christian practice, as founded on the principles and precepts of the New Testament.

25. It is deemed unnecessary to trace the historical evidence into the fifth and succeeding centuries. In every step of the progress downwards, the testimony becomes more and more crowded, by Christian writers, by the writings of the heretics and by those opposed to Christianity. In the early part of the fourth century, the Christian religion was acknowledged in the palace of the Cæsars, and in the Roman Empire, the mighty structure of the Pagan Idolatry fell to rise no more.

26. From the days of the Apostles numerous Christian churches have existed in all parts of the civilized world. Multitudes of all ranks, abandoned their idol worship, and embraced the pure principles of the Gospel. Now, in the continued evidence of these Christian Churches, and in the concurrence of the multitudes who professed the Christian faith, we have the most conclusive evidence to the truth of the Gospel history. It is the unbroken and the daily testimony of hundreds of thousands of unexceptionable witnesses in all parts of the world. In their local and dispersed situations, in all ages, combination and collusion, for the purposes of forgery and deception, were impracticable ; and by their united and continued testimony a chain of evidence, the most conclusive, the most perfect, is established from the first rise of Christianity to the present time.

IV. NEW TESTAMENT DIVINELY INSPIRED.

27. The writers of the New Testament not only claim to have had perfect knowledge of the things which they saw and heard and taught, but they go further, and in all these claim to have been under a divine and infallible guidance. In reference to the historical facts, they assert "that they were guided by a divine direction, that God Himself taught them all things, and brought all things to their remembrance, whatsoever Jesus Christ had said unto them." In reference to precepts and doctrines, they assert "that they were such as they had received of the Lord," that they spoke "not in the words which man's wisdom teacheth, but which the Holy Ghost teacheth"; that these things "were not received by man but by the revelation of Jesus Christ." In a word, they claim to have recorded a Divine Revelation as delivered to them "by the wisdom of the Living God."

28. Before proceeding to examine the evidence on which the New Testament writers rest this high claim, it is proper to examine what the claim itself really is, and how it applies to these writings, as consisting of history, precepts and prophecy. On this subject much has been written, and often have attempts at explanation made it more obscure. We are told of plenary inspiration, of an inspiration of superintendency, of a plenary superintendent inspiration, of an inspiration of suggestion, of elevation, etc., etc. It is believed that the use of these different terms is unnecessary and injurious; and that they only darken counsel by words without knowledge.

29. On turning to the pages of the record itself to see what this claim is, we find it expressed and referred to in a great variety of ways. Sometimes the expressions are general and indefinite. The fact that the communication was divine, is distinctly asserted, but not the manner in which it was made to them. "On the day of Pentecost the disciples were all filled with the Holy Ghost, and began to speak with toher tongues as the Spirit gave them utterance." Acts ii, 4. "For I have received of the Lord that which also I delivered unto you." I Cor. xi, 23. "For I neither received it by man, neither was I taught it, but by the revelation of Jesus Christ." Gal. v, 12. "Holy men spake as they were moved by the Holy Ghost." II Pet. i, 21. In some instances the expressions are more definite, and we are informed how the revelation was made. When the apostles were cast into prison, the angel of the Lord sets them free, and directs them "to go, stand and speak in the temple to people all the words of this life." Acts v, 19, 20. "The angel of the Lord spake unto Philip, saying, Arise go towards the south." Acts viii, 26. "The angel of the Lord stood by Paul and spoke to him," Acts xxvii, 23. "And again an angel appeared to John, and explained and revealed to him things to come." Rev. xxii, 16. "The Holy Ghost said, separate me Barnabas and Paul, for the work whereunto I have called them." Acts xiii, 2. Unto the third heavens was the apostle of the Gentiles caught up, and heard unspeakable words whether in the body or out of the body, He did not Himself know. II Cor. xii, 1-3. John, the forerunner of Jesus Christ, at the baptism of His Lord, and the three disciples on the Mount heard a Voice from heaven, saying, "This is my Be-

loved Son in whom I am well pleased." Mat. iii, 17 and xvii, 5; II Pet. i, 17, 18.

A great part of the New Testament message was revealed by Jesus Christ Himself to His disciples. During years of familiar and most endearing intercourse, He revealed and expounded to them the things of His kingdom. From heaven He descended, and in brightness above the mid-day sun, spoke to the violent persecutor of His people, from thenceforth called to be one of His most distinguished witnesses. Acts ix, 1–20. To the same apostle He again appeared in a vision, encouraging and strengthening him. Acts xviii, 9. To him who leaned on his breast at supper, He again appeared in the Isle of Patmos; but so glorious, that the beloved disciple fell at His feet as dead. Rev. i, 17.

30. In all these rich and varied expressions of the New Testament writers, we are taught to consider them as having delivered to us a message from God. That this message in all its parts consists of entire truth, and of such truth as it was the will and good pleasure of God should be revealed to us by them. The communication of these truths to them is in the message itself called "Divine Inspiration."* This means nothing more nor less than the Divine Revelation, or communication, of these truths to their minds, and thereby enabling them, without error or mistake, to speak and write the things, thus by them received, whether relating to prophecy, moral precepts or historical facts.

31. The Divine Inspiration claimed by these writers, as far as it respects prophecy and moral precepts, is

---

*Theopneustos, I Tim. iii, 16.

easily understood; but how it applies to historical facts is not so apparent, and hence, as already noticed, the diversity of terms applied to this subject. It is asked, where is the necessity of Divine Inspiration, when a competent witness, in relating a fact, speaks from personal knowledge? There is no doubt but in such a case the truth may be told without Divine Inspiration; and that a historical fact recorded under divine guidance, and one recorded without it, may be both equally true. But those to whom the relation of the fact is given have not the same certainty of its truth in both cases. In one, there is the possibility of forgetfulness, the possibility of misapprehension and of error, the possibility that the relation of the fact itself is not necessary; the other is beyond any such possibility. The one testimony is human, the other is Divine.

32. Another inquiry of some moment belongs to this branch of the subject. Does this Divine Inspiration extend to the words, or only to the thoughts or minds of the writers?

Every one who is capable of examining the New Testament in the original language will perceive that it is not written in the pure Greek of Xenophon or Plato. It is Hebraic Greek, or such as was used by the Jews when they spoke or wrote in Greek. The original Greek, also, or even a faithful translation shows a diversity of style amongst these writers. We find also that in relating the same facts there is seldom a verbal agreement.

It is evident, therefore, from the language in which these books were written, that of Hebraic Greek, from the diversity of style of the different writers, and from the verbal differences in the relation of facts.

that, to some extent at least, these writers were left to the resources of their own minds. But we must remember that the clear perception of knowledge enabled them to express it clearly, either in speaking or writing.

The foregoing remarks are illustrated, and indeed are embraced, in another consideration. In translating the New Testament from the Greek into another language, if the translation be faithful, the Divine Inspiration is not lost in the change of words or idioms; it is still a Divine Revelation, though spoken in another tongue. So in secular affairs. The testimony of witnesses admitted to be honest and competent, though spoken in a language unknown to the court and jury, will yet be the foundation for the judgment and verdict of that court and jury even in cases of life and death. Here, of course, the court and jury will first be well assured that the testimony has been faithfully translated.

Whilst, therefore, on the one hand, we are not to consider the words nor the arrangement of the words as being divinely inspired, so, on the other hand, we are not warranted, by anything contained in the message itself, in concluding that no limits were assigned on these points to the minds of the writers. On the contrary, whatever discretion or latitude was allowed, they claim distinctly to have delivered their message, not in the words of human wisdom but in the words as taught by a Divine Teacher. I Cor. ii—3, 13.

33. Having thus considered what Divine Inspiration is, let us now examine the evidence by which the claim to it is supported.

We have already seen (No. 11) that these writers gave the highest evidence of sincerity by their holy and blameless lives, by their sufferings and by their submitting voluntarily to martyrdom in the support of the truth of the things related. But one of the things thus related by them is the fact that they spake not of themselves but as it was revealed to them. They tell us that they heard a Voice from heaven saying, "This is my Beloved Son in whom I am well pleased." They tell us that on the day of Pentecost they were all filled with the Holy Ghost, and began to speak with other tongues as the Spirit gave them utterance. They tell us that such and such things were revealed to them by the Lord, and that they delivered His message as they received it. From the very nature of the facts recorded every argument and every consideration, which proves the record to be genuine and authentic, proves its Divine Inspiration.

34. The miracles performed by Jesus Christ are conclusive proof that his was a divine mission. As such he appeals to them (John v, 36); and as such the sincere enquirers after the truth considered them; (John iii, 2 and ix, 31). The writers of the New Testament also appeal to the miracles performed by them as full proof that their message was divine (Acts v, 32); and these appeals are conclusive; they are beyond the reach of cavil; the miracles set the broad seal of heaven to the divine mission of the Lord Jesus Christ, and to the truth of the testimony of the apostles.

35. The enemies of Divine Revelation have felt the force of this part of the Christian argument, and their utmost efforts have been made to lessen or evade it. Down to the time of the Emperor Julian, the opposers of Christianity ascribed the miracles to

magic. Neither Celsus, Porphyry nor Julian denied
the fact that the miracles recorded in the New Testament had been performed. But they contended that
Jesus, when in Egypt, had learned magic, and these
were the fruits of His skill. "Let us grant," says
Celsus, "that they were performed ; must we not say
that these are the artifices of wicked and miserable
men?" "Jesus," says Julian, "did nothing in his
lifetime worthy of remembrance, unless any one
thinks it a mighty matter to heal lame and blind
people, and exorcise demoniacs in the valleys of
Bethsaida and Bethany." One skeptic of modern
date has contended that, from the nature of the fact
itself, as being contrary to our experience, no proof
could establish a miracle. And the infidels of our
day content themselves with a naked denial of their
existence.

The objections of the heathen opposers are now no
further worthy of notice than to show how the ground
of opposition has been shifted since that time. The
sophistry of Hume and his followers never deceived a
sincere enquirer after truth. If we are to believe
nothing but what we see and hear, for the objection
amounts to that, then is our knowledge small indeed.
To this day the writer of these remarks never saw or
felt an earthquake, or a waterspout, or a volcanic
eruption. It is contrary to all his experience that
either of these ever existed. But the principles of
human testimony are not contrary to his experience,
and, therefore, he has no doubt that these things have
been seen and felt by others. In common with those
who preceded them, the Carlisles, the Wrights and
the Owens of the present time contend that human
reason is sufficient in all cases. Yet, on this subject,

they will not reason. If they are invited to an examination of the historical evidence of the New Testament, they answer by naked assertion or coarse and
contemptible ridicule and invective. While they
pursue this course, argument is of no avail; reason
itself is useless; so to him who is blind, and to him
who obstinately and wilfully shuts his eyes, the light
is equally useless.

PROPHECY.

36. If prophecy exist at all, every one will con-
cede that it is an evidence of Divine Revelation ; and
that the knowledge of future events is a knowledge
derived immediately from heaven. If the fact of any
one prophecy and its fulfilment be proved, the fact
of the Divine Inspiration of the agent announcing the
prophecy is also proved.

37. A few only of the numerous prophecies contained in the New Testament are selected to illustrate
this branch of the subject.

E. We find the Lord Jesus Christ informing his
disciples beforehand that he would be betrayed to the
chief priests and scribes ; that they would condemn
him to death, and deliver him to the gentiles ; and
that, after the most insulting and cruel treatment, he
would be crucified, and after three days rise again
from the dead. Matt. xvi, 21; xvii, 22; xx, 18–19 ;
Mark viii, 31; ix, 31 ; x, 33–34; Luke ix, 22 ; xviii,
31–33. All these predictions to the very letter were
fulfilled in the sufferings, death and resurrection of
our blessed Lord.

F. The descent of the Holy Ghost upon the
apostles, and the power of working miracles and
speaking with other tongues are distinctly foretold,

and the full accomplishment of all these distinctly
recorded. Luke xxiv, 49 ; Mark xvi, 17–18; Acts ii.

G. The destruction of Jerusalem and its celebrated
temple, the period when this awful event would take
place, the signs which would precede it, the dreadful
miseries and calamities, and the total ruin that would
then befall the Jewish nation, are clearly, distinctly
and minutely predicted. Mat. xxiii, 37–38 and xxiv,
2–21 ; Mark xiii, 2–22 ; Luke xiii, 34–35 and xix, 23
and xxi, 6–24. In the history of Josephus, and in
the Roman and other historians, of that and later
periods, and in the history of the homeless, fugitive
Jews, scattered through all nations for 1800 years,
we have the full and distinct account of the perfect
fulfilment of this most remarkable and stupendous
prediction.

THE OLD TESTAMENT GENUINE AND AUTHENTIC.

38. The writings of the Old Testament, although
usually bound in one volume, and like the New
Testament, by many considered as but one book, consist of thirty-nine different books, written by nearly
as many different authors, at different times during a
period of more than a thousand years, from the death
of Moses, A. M. 2555 to the close of the prophecy of
Malachi in A. M. 3580.

39. The best account we have of these writers is
contained in the books themselves and in the books
of the New Testament, and it would be an interesting
employment to draw the character of each writer as
given in those authentic records. But here that
would be out of place, and it must suffice to observe
that amongst them we find statesmen rich in the

experience and wisdom acquired in the government of mighty empires, distinguished warriors, powerful kings, humble shepherds, poets, prophets, and historians, and embracing talents and arguments, modes of thought and expression as various, as were their learning, natural abilities, occupation or employment.

40. We have the uncontradicted tradition of the Jews, whose political history these books record, to their genuineness and truth. From the time the first of them was written, their care and preservation were assigned to a particular tribe, specially set apart for that and similar purposes. On their face they have every mark of genuine and authentic records. They contain many things to the disadvantage of the nation ; they abound in particulars of dates, places and persons ; but above all, they record the final deliverance from bondage, and the written laws and ordinances of a whole people, existing at the present time, and adhering to and regulated by these laws and ordinances.

41. It will scarcely be contended by any that the Declaration of Independence, the Constitution of the United States, and the Laws of Congress did not exist from the time they purport to have existed. This illustration in part, has already been used in reference to the books of the New Testament (No. 17). As it respects the five books of Moses the parallel is complete. The 4th day of July is the birthday of one people, from the oppression of Great Britain ; the 15th day of the month Abib, is the birthday of the other people from the bondage of Egypt ; and these days are annually celebrated by each people respectively. The constitution and laws of the

United States have, since their first existence, been received by the people of the United States, and by them are our people at this time regulated and governed. The laws, ordinances and ceremonies given by Moses to the Hebrews, were also received by that people, and by them are the Jews, at this time, regulated and governed. By reference to the cases already considered (Nos. 16, 26) it will be seen that the supposition of forgery and falsehood in either of these cases is impossible and absurd.

42. The nations existing at the time the books of the Old Testament were written have all disappeared. These books, and these alone, give us the history of the rise and fall of Edom, Moab, Ammon, Midian, Philistia and of Amalik. Ancient Egypt is now no more; Assyria, Nineveh and Tyre have for ages ceased to exist, and many generations have passed away since the once great and mighty Babylon has been swept with the besom of desolation; their records, their histories, their monuments have shared the same fate—destruction and oblivion have passed upon all. With the solitary exception of one Jewish historian, when we leave the pages of the Old Testament writings, fable, tradition, and a few scattered fragments of the historians of later nations, are all that remain. The history of Josephus is the only one which speaks of the times and the things related in these books, and he wrote fourteen hundred years after the first, and four hundred years after the last of the Old Testament writers. But it will be shown hereafter that this absence of historical evidence is abundantly supplied by proof of another kind, the most decisive and conclusive.

THE OLD TESTAMENT DIVINELY INSPIRED.

43. *Miracles.*—The writers of the Old Testament claim to have written under the guidance of Divine Inspiration, and they prove the truth of their claim by miracles and prophecy. If it be admitted that the claim to both or to either is well founded, the question is settled by that admission. Let us examine them separately.

The miracles performed by Moses hold the first place as to time and greatness. Of these, it might be sufficient to observe that they are recorded in the same books which contain the constitution, laws and ordinances of the Hebrew nation. If it has been proved (Nos. 40, 41) that these laws have existed from the time they are said to have existed, the fact that the miracles were then performed is also proved. But as this point is of acknowledged importance, let us examine it more particularly. These miracles are: That for the deliverance of Israel, ten destructive plagues, at the word of Moses, were brought upon the Egyptians; that an arm of the Arabian Gulf was divided, and the whole host of Israel passed through on dry land; that a cloud by day and a pillar of fire by night went before them; that in the desert manna from heaven was their daily food, water from the barren rock was their daily drink for the space of forty years; that while encamped at Mount Sinai they witnessed a most astonishing, awful and stupendous display of Divine power, majesty and glory. These and other miracles are said to have been witnessed by a whole nation, by the entire population, consisting of six hundred thousand men, besides women and children, and a mixed multitude from other nations.

Now it will be admitted, or can easily be proved, that this same people exist at the present day, and that they firmly believe that these miracles were performed, and seen by their fathers, as we find them recorded in the books of Moses.

If the account of these miracles is false, and is a forgery, it must be an imposition of the age when they are said to have been performed, or an imposition of some subsequent age. But it could not be the first, because a whole people had personal knowledge of the subject; it relates to facts about which they could not be mistaken or deceived, and by no possibility could they be brought to believe what they knew to be false. Neither could the account be an imposition of a later period. The books which record the miracles contain also the constitution and laws of the whole people. They claim to have been written at the time of that deliverance, and assert that the generation then existing witnessed all the facts, and submitted to and were regulated by the laws there recorded. Now, suppose all this to be a forgery first brought forward 100 or 500 years after the Exodus. Is it possible that the generation then existing could be induced to believe that for 100 or 500 years they and their fathers had been governed by peculiar laws, of which they had never heard till that time? Or that numerous and stupendous miracles had been performed in the presence of their forefathers, of which also they had never heard before? The statement of these questions shows the supposition to be impossible and absurd.

44. *Prophecies.* — The numerous and astonish-

ing prophecies of the Old Testament prove its divine origin. A few of these only can be here noticed.

Of Ismael, the son of Abraham, and the father of the tribes of Arabia, it was foretold before his birth that he should be a wild ass man :—That his hand should be against every man, and every man's hand against him—and that he should be the father of a great nation. The accomplishment of the prophecy has been written in the history of this remarkable people for the last four thousand years. In every age and to this day these tribes are as free as the wild ass of the desert. "Their house is in the wilderness and the barren land their dwelling." They have repelled the greatest efforts, of Eygpt, of Assyria and of Rome, made against them in the days of the greatest strength and power of those kingdoms ; and as in former times, so at this day "they scorn the multitude of the cities, their hand is still against every man, and the hand of every man is still against them."

45. The prophecies relating to the property of Abraham, Isaac and Jacob are numerous ; many have been fulfilled, some are now fulfilling, and some are yet future. Let us examine one delivered by Moses three thousand two hundred years ago. "And the Lord shall scatter thee among all people from the one end of the earth even unto the other ; and among all these nations shalt thou find no ease, neither shall the sole of thy foot have rest ; but the Lord shall give thee there a trembling heart, and failing of eyes, and sorrow of mind ; and thy life shall hang in doubt before thee ; and thou shalt fear day and night, and shalt have none assurance for thy life ; and thou shalt become an astonishment, a proverb and a bye-word,

among all nations whither the Lord shall lead thee." Deut. xxviii, 64–67.

These few lines contain the history of the Jews for the last seventeen hundred years ; and no historian could describe their actual condition during that period, and as now existing in language more appropriate than that used by the prophet thirty centuries ago.   The wonderful accomplishment of the prophecy comes home to our personal knowledge.   We know that this people, separate and distinct from all others, are scattered among all nations ; and we know that their condition in every country is here truly described.   And what is most extraordinary, and apparently impossible, is that our own blessed country, this enlightened land of equal rights, this home of the oppressed and persecuted of all nations, forms no exception ! Even with us, public sentiment is against them, and proscribes and persecutes them in a thousand ways ; in many things dearest to the heart of man, our equal right to them are but a name ; and altho' the existence of this fact is not honorable to us, yet we do know that the Jew is still a proverb and a bye-word amongst us.   Their existence as a distinct people, thus dispersed, and thus persecuted, is a standing miracle, which all the infidel philosophers in the world cannot contradict, nor on their principles explain.

46. In the year B.C. 975, we find the union of the Hebrew states broken, and the tribes of Israel existing under two separate and hostile governments. The able but ambitious and profligate ruler of the ten tribes, acting on the councils of a crooked worldly policy, had erected places of worship in his own dominions, to prevent his people from going to the

territories of the rival where the temple was built, and where by the law of Moses the whole people were required to assemble. In this state of hostile rivalry a prophet from Judah, in the presence of Jeroboam, predicted "that a child born unto the house of David, Josiah by name, should defile his altar, and burn the bones of dead men upon it," I Kings xiii, 2. This prophecy could not take place until the power of two tribes, governed by the house of David, should be extended over the other ten, which at that time was most unlikely. Yet in three hundred and fifty years we have the record of its fulfilment to the very letter. II Kings xxiii, 15.

47. About the year B.C. 600 we find the kingdom of Judah under subjection to the king of Babylon. Part of the people had been carried captive into Assyria, and part were in India under Zedekiah, the tributary of Nebuchadnezzer. After a reign of eleven years of oppression and injustice Zedekiah rebelled against the king of Babylon. At this time the prophet Jeremiah resided in Jerusalem, and the prophet Ezekiel in the land of Assyria. Each predicted the result of the coming contest, and particularly what would befall the Hebrew monarch. An apparent direct contradiction between these two prophets afforded abundant ground of cavil to the persecuting infidels, and time-serving courtiers of that day. Jeremiah predicted that Zedekiah should see the king of Babylon, and be carried to Babylon. Ezekiel, that he should not see Babylon. Jeremiah, that he should die in peace, and be buried after the manner of his ancestors. Ezekiel, that he should die at Babylon, Jer. xxxii, 1–5 ; Ez. xii, 13. But the history shewed both prophets to have been right, and that there was

no error in the Spirit by which they spoke. "So they took the king, and brought him up to the king of Babylon to Reblah; and they gave judgments upon him. And they slew the sons of Zedekiah before his eyes, and put out the eyes of Zedekiah, and bound him with fetters of brass, and carried him to Babylon." II Kings xxv, 6–7.

48. Eygpt, Ethiopia, Nineveh and Tyre were at different times the most powerful states of antiquity; and Edom, Moab, Ammon and Philistia were communities of more or less importance and all of long standing. All these were the objects of minute, definite and specific prophecy; and their history and their present desolation shew that the predictions of their fate, were given by Him who knows the end from the beginning.

49. Babylon was long the seat of power and dominion in the eastern world; and there also was the seat of commerce, of manufactures, and of the mechanic and fine arts. Learning and science took up their abode there. Her buildings, her hanging gardens, her walls and brazen gates have in all ages been the wonder of the world. In the year B.C. 550 this empire was in the full height of strength and power under an able statesman, the first warrior of that age. How strange to those who would neither believe nor regard, must have appeared the predictions of the utter ruin, and perpetual desolation of such a mighty empire. But years in advance had the God of Israel by his prophets foretold her overthrow, and placed on record the very name of her conquerer. And as if to leave the infidels of the present day without excuse for saying that these predictions were forgeries after the events had taken place, the pen of Divine Inspira-

tion has described the perpetual ruin, which yet rests upon this glory of kingdoms ; and thus from age to age, has a standing miracle been exhibited to the world, which stamps the record with the seal of Divine truth, and sets infidelity and cavil at defiance.

"Babylon shall become a possession for the bit- terns, and pools of water, the wild beast of the desert shall dwell there ; and the owls shall dwell therein. Babylon the glory of kingdoms, shall become heaps, a dwelling place for dragons, an astonishment, and an living without an inhabitant ; she shall sink and shall not rise from the evil that I shall bring upon her. As God overthrew Sodom and Gomorah, and the neighbouring cities thereof, so shall no man dwell there, neither shall any son of man dwell therein. It shall be no more inhabited forever ; neither shall it be dwelt in from generation to generation. Neither shall the Arabian pitch tent there ; neither shall the shepherds make their fold there. But wild beasts of the desert shall be there, and their houses shall be full of doleful creatures, and owls shall dwell there, and dragons in their pleasant palaces." Isa. xlv, 1–3 ; Jer. l, 39–40, and li, 26, 37, 64 ; Isa. xiii, 19–22, 50.

The prophet Daniel was preëminent in wisdom and piety, and the most distinguished statesman of the age. Under the greatest Babylonian monarch and his successors, and under Cyrus and Darius, from his youth to extreme old age, we find him filling, with purity and ability, the most responsible trusts in the greatest empire in the world. Whilst yet a young man he acquired the well-founded confidence of Nebuchadnezzer ; and his distinguished merits and abilities insured to him the lasting friendship and esteem of Cyrus and of Darius. In his writings the transfer, by conquest, of the empire to the Medes and Persians, the subversion of that power by the Grecians, the division into four parts which followed the death of the Grecian conquerer, and the rise of the Roman government, were all foretold in language so definite, that the historian of these great events has but filled up the specific outline of the prophet. Dan. ii, 39–40, and vii, 17–24, and viii and ix.

This series of remarkable prophecies has very much annoyed and pressed the advocates of infidelity. Distinguished and able men of that party have given reasons for their unbelief directly in conflict with each other. The learned and sagacious Porphyry, in the third century, contended that, between the prophecies of Daniel and the record of history, the parallel was so complete that the predictions were forgeries of a period after the events had occurred. Jefferson, however, in the nineteenth century, thought otherwise ; but equally unwilling to admit the agency of Divine influence, he contends, "that the whole of the prophecies were fumes of the most disordered imagination; that it was only by the aid of allegories, figures, types, and other tricks and words, that the events now and then turning up in the course of ages could be accommodated to these vague rhapsodies."* No argument is shaken by naked assertion or indecent cavils ; and the cause must be desperate which affords its ablest advocates no other ground of defense. In the present case, the operation of the one shows that he had compared the prophecy with the historical evidence of its fulfilment ; but instead of going one step further, and examining the evidence for the

---

* Jefferson Mem., vol. iv, p. 325, let. 153.

time when the prophecy was written, he rests the argument on an assertion which is contradicted by the clearest testimony. The contemptible cavil of the other shews only that he had not examined the subject at all. It is just what might be expected from one who declares that "he rested on the writings of Priestly and Middleton as the basis of his truth."* A poor basis truly, and a strange faith which thus rests contented in ignorance and unbelief.

51. The series of prophecies in the Old Testament respecting the Messiah, and their accomplishment in the person of Jesus Christ, as recorded in the New, furnishes to every lover of truth a field of most interesting inquiry, and leads to results on which the human mind can rest with perfect certainty. If these prophecies have been fulfiled, they prove the divine origin of the Old Testament. If they have been fulfiled in Jesus Christ, they prove Him to have been the promised Messiah. Our Lord Himself challenges investigation on this point. "Search the Scriptures, for they are they that testify of me." Again and again do the New Testament writers assert, that in the instances they were then recording, the ancient prophecies were fulfiled. To reach the truth on this most important subject, no great or splendid talents are necessary. It is level to the capacity of all. Here is the prophecy ; there is what is said to be the fulfilment. Are they parallel? Do they correspond with each other? A few instances, as specimens merely, will be here noticed.

H. Where the Messiah should be born.

Prophecy.—"And thou Bethlehem Ephratah,

---

* Jefferson's Mem., vol. iv, p. 206, let. 112.

though thou be little among the thousands of Judah, yet out of thee shall he come forth unto me, that is to be ruler in Israel; whose going forth has been of old, from the days of eternity." Micah v, 2.

Fulfilment.—"And Joseph went forth from Galilee, out of the City of Nazareth, into Judea, unto the city of David, which is called Bethlehem, (because he was of the house and lineage of David,) to be taxed, with Mary, his espoused wife, being great with child. And so it was, that while they were there the days were accomplished that she should be delivered. And she brought forth her first-born son, and wrapped him in swaddling clothes, and laid him in a manger; because there was no room for them in the inn." Luke ii, 4-7.

I. The Messiah should be born of a virgin.

Prophecy.—"Therefore the Lord himself shall give you a sign; behold a virgin shall conceive, and bear a son, and shall call his name Immanuel." Isa. vii, 14.

Fulfilment.—"But while he thought on these things, behold the angel of the Lord appeared unto him in a dream, saying, Joseph, thou son of David, fear not to take unto thee Mary thy wife, for that which is conceived in her is of the Holy Ghost. And she shall bring forth a son, and thou shalt call his name Jesus: for He shall save his people from their sins." Mat. i, 20-21; also Luke i, 26-35.

J. The Messiah should be God and man.

Prophecy.—"For unto us a child is born, unto us a son is given, and the government shall be upon his shoulder; and his name shall be called Wonderful Counsellor, the mighty God, the everlasting Father, the Prince of Peace." Is. ix, 6; also Ps. ii, 7 and cx, 1; Mec. v, 2.

Fulfilment.—In the beginning was the Word, and the Word was with God, and the Word was God. And the Word was made flesh and dwelt amongst us, and we beheld his glory, the glory as of the only begotten of the Father full of grace and truth." John i, 1, 14. Whose are the fathers, and of whom as concerning the flesh Christ came, who is over all, God blessed for ever, Amen." Rom. ix, 5. "For in Him dwelleth all the fulness of the Godhead bodily." Col. ii, 9. "But now ye seek to kill me, a man that hath told you the truth." John viii, 40. "This is the true God and eternal life." I John v, 5-20; also Heb. i, 1-8; Mat. xxii, 42-44 and i, 23.

K. Messiah should be destitute of outward power.

Prophecy.—"He is despised and rejected of men; a man of sorrow and acquainted with grief; and we hid as it were our faces from him; he was despised and we esteemed him not." Is. liii, 3.

Fulfilment.—"And Jesus said unto him, Foxes have holes, and the birds of the air have nests; but the son of man hath not where to lay his head." Luke ix, 58. "For ye know the grace of our Lord Jesus Christ, that, though He was rich yet for your sakes He became poor, that ye through His poverty might be rich." II Cor. viii, 9.

L. His Mission and Doctrines confirmed by miracles.

Prophecy.—"Then the eyes of the blind shall be opened, and the ears of the deaf shall be unstopped; then shall the lame leap as an hare, and the tongue of the dumb shall sing." Is. xxxv, 5-6.

"I the Lord have called thee in righteousness, and will hold thine hand, and will keep thee, and give thee for a covenant, for a light to the Gentiles; to open the eyes of the blind, to bring out the prisoners from the prison, and them that set in darkness out of the prison house." Is. xlii, 6–7.

Fulfilment.—"And Jesus said unto them, Go and shew John again those things which ye do hear and see ; the blind receive their sight, and the lame walk, the lepers are cleansed, the dead are raised up, and the poor have the gospel preached unto them." Mat. xi, 4–5 ; also Mat. iv, 23–24 and xv, 31 ; Luke viii, 54.

M. Messiah should suffer insult and cruel mockings.

Prophecy.—"But I am a worm and no man ; a reproach of men, and despised of the people. All they that see me laugh me to scorn, they shoot out the lip, they shake the head saying, He trusted in the Lord that He would deliver Him ; let Him deliver Him seeing he delighted in Him." Ps. xxii, 7–8.

Fulfilment.—"And they that passed by reviled Him wagging their heads, and saying Thou that destroyest the temple and buildest it in three days, save Thyself. If Thou be the Son of God come down from the cross. Likewise also the chief priests mocking Him, with the scribes and elders, said, He saved others Himself He cannot save. If He be the king of Israel let Him now come down from the cross and we will believe in Him. He trusted in God ; let Him deliver Him now if He will have Him ; for He said 'I am the Son of God.'" Mat. xxvii, 39–43 ; also Mark xv, 31–32 ; Luke xxiii, 35–36.

N. Messiah should suffer death for the sins of others.

Prophecy.—"But He was wounded for our transgressions, He was bruised for our iniquities ; the chastisement of our fear was upon Him ; and with His stripes we are healed. . . . He was taken from prison and from judgment ; and who shall declare His generation ? for He was cut off out of the land of the living : for the transgression of my people was He stricken. . . . He poured out His soul unto the death ; and He was numbered with transgressors ; and He bore the sins of many, and made intercession for the transgressor." Is. liii, 5, 8, 12.

Fulfilment.—"And it was the third hour and they crucified Him. And with Him they crucify two thieves, the one on His right hand, and the other on His left. And the Scripture was fulfiled, which saith, and He was numbered with the transgressors." Mark xv, 25-28. "Who His own self bore our sins in His own body on the tree, that we being dead to sins, should live unto righteousness, by whose stripes ye were healed." I Pet. ii, 24; also Mat. viii, 17 ; John i, 29 ; Heb. ix, 28.

O. The manner of the death and burial of the Messiah.

Prophecy.—"And His grave was appointed with the wicked ; But with the rich man was His tomb." Isa. liii, 9.*

Fulfilment.—"When the even was come, there came a rich man of Asemathea named Joseph,

---

*Bishop Lowth translation.

ויהן את רשעים קברו
ואת עשיר במתיו

The parallel passages, Deut. xxxii, 13 ; Is. lviii, 14 ; Amos iv, 13 ; Mic. i, 3 ; Isa. xiv, 14 ; Job. ix, 8, shew that במתי signifies heights or high places. From II Chron. xxxii, 33, and Isa. xxii, 16, the Jewish graves are shown to have been in high situations. Notes Bishop Lowth's Isaiah.

who also himself was Jesus' disciple; he went
to Pilate and begged the body of Jesus. Then
Pilate commanded the body to be delivered. And
when Joseph had taken the body, he wrapped
it in a clean linen cloth, and laid it in his own
new tomb, which he had hewn out of the rock;
and he rolled a great stone to the door of the
sepulchre and departed." Mat. xxvii, 57–60.

P. The Messiah should arise from the dead and
ascend to heaven.

Prophecy.—"For Thou wilt not leave my soul in
the grave, neither wilt Thou suffer Thine holy one to
see corruption." Ps. xvi, 10. "Thou hast ascended
up on high; Thou hast led captivity captive." Ps.
lxviii, 18.

Fulfilment.—"And the angel said unto them, fear
ye not, for I know that ye seek Jesus which was
crucified. He is not here; for he has risen as He said,
"Come see the place where the Lord lay." Mat. xxviii,
5–6. "To whom also He showed Himself alive after
His passion, by many infallible proofs, being seen of
them forty days, and speaking of the things pertain-
ing to the kingdom of God. And when He had
spoken these things, while they beheld, He was taken
up; and a bright cloud received Him out of their
sight." Acts i, 3–9; also, Acts ii, 31 and xiii, 35; Luke
xxiv, 5–6, 51; Mark xvi, 19.

52. The distinct testimony of Jesus Christ and His
apostles to the truth and Divine Inspiration of the
Old Testament, is of itself conclusive and most
abundantly supplies any want of historical evidence,
occasioned by the loss and destruction of the ancient
records of other nation. . . . From numerous
references the following are selected: Mat. xi, 13

and xxii, 40-43 ; Luke xvi, 16 and xx, 42 and xxiv,
25-44 ; Acts i, 20 and iii, 22 and vii, 35-37 and xxvi,
22 and xxviii, 23 ; Rom. x, 5 ; II Cor. iii, 7-15 ; II
Tim. iii, 14-17 ; Heb. vii, 14 and x, 28.

  V. Internal evidences.

  53. In considering what are usually called the internal evidences, it is proper distinctly to disclaim
all intention of bringing the doctrines and precepts
of the Bible to be judged of by the fallible standard
of human reason.   Much injury has resulted from
this practice, and it cannot be too carefully guarded
against the councils, and the purpose of the Divine
mind,—what is proper for the Almighty to do, and
what is proper for Him to reveal, lie all beyond the
safe legitimate exercise of our reasoning powers.
Giving these considerations, however, their full weight,
it will be found that a careful examination of the
writings of the Old and New Testaments will lead to
very satisfactory conclusions.

  54. The works of Creation and Providence reveal
to us much of the power, wisdom and goodness of God.
But it is in the Bible alone that we have revealed to
us His true character and perfections.   "God is a
Spirit and they shall worship Him, must worship in
Spirit and in truth." John iv, 24.   "He is the King
eternal, immortal invisible, and the only wise God."
I Tem, i, 17.   "He is the Father of Light, in
whom there is no variableness, neither shadow of
turning." Jam. i, 17.   "His greatness is unsearchable." Ps. cxlv, 3.   "And God said unto Moses, I
am that I am; and he said, Thus shalt thou say unto
the children of Isrsel, I am, hath sent me unto you."
Ex. iii, 14.   "He that loveth not knoweth not God,
for God is Love." I John iv, 8.   "And the Lord

passed by before him, and proclaimed the Lord, the Lord God, merciful and gracious, long suffering and abundant in goodness and truth keeping mercy for thousands, forgiving iniquity, transgression and sin, and that will by no means clean the guilty." Ex. xxxiv, 6–7 ; also Col. i, 16 ; Dan. iv, 34–35.

A comparison is most confidently invited between these extracts, which might be continued to great extent, and anything that ever was written in any age and nation, not having the Bible.

55. As matters of fact we are quite able to compare the system of Divine truth as revealed in the Holy Scriptures with the different systems of religion which do now exist ; or which in any prior age have existed in the world. None who have the Bible are now found to advocate the ancient or the modern superstitions of heathenism. Modern infidelity indeed contends for the sufficiency of human reason. The truths of Divine Revelation, which the human mind in a long course of ages had not discovered are now used and boasted of, as the productions of enlightened reason. If this were so, how did it happen that these truths were known to the sages and philosophers, of Eygpt, of Babylon, of Greece and Rome ? It is between the writings of these sages and philosophers aided by their consuls, their kings and their emperors on the one side, and the writings of the shepherds, the herd-men and the fishermen of Bethlehem, of Tekoa, and of Gallilee on the other, that the comparison fairly rests. Compare then the systems produced by this array of wealth, human learning and intelligence, with the truths of the Bible, and unless Divine Inspiration be admitted, on no principle known to us can we explain the difference.

56. From the beginning to the end of the books of the Old and New Testament we find " Holiness to the Lord" written as with a sunbeam on every page; most appropriately, indeed, when these records are bound in one are they called the Holy Bible. There we find that God is most Holy, that heaven is a holy place, and all its inhabitants are holy ; that the law of God is holy, that the road to heaven is a holy road, and that without holiness no man shall see the Lord. "And one cried to another, and said, Holy, holy, holy, is the Lord God of Hosts; the whole earth is full of his glory." Isa. vi, 3. "Be ye therefore holy, for I am holy." Ex. xi, 45. "God sitteth upon the throne of his holiness." Ps. xlvii, 8. "And there shall in no wise enter into it anything that defileth, or worketh abomination, or maketh a lie." Rev. xxi, 27. "For thus saith the High and the Lofty One that inhabiteth eternity, whose name is Holy, I dwell in the high and holy place with him also that is of a contrite and humble spirit, to revive the spirit of the humble, and to revive the heart of the contrite ones." Is. lvii, 15. "Wherefore the law is holy ; and the commandment holy, and just, and good." Rom. vii, 12–13. "Worship the Lord in the beauty of holiness." I Chr. xvi, 29. "And an highway shall be there, and a way, and it shall be called the way of holiness ; the unclean shall not pass over it; the wayfaring men, though fools, shall not err therein." Is. xxv, 8.

The holiness and purity revealed in the Bible, and thus required by all its precepts, afford the most convincing and satisfying evidence of its heavenly origin. Such a book cannot be the work of wicked men,—purity and holiness is the very opposite of all they say or do. Neither can it be the work of good men,—because they would not attempt to deceive the world by a fabrication. Infidelity has been so pressed by these considerations, that its leaders have been forced to deny the holiness of the Divine Record. "The God of the Jews" says one "would be deemed a very indifferent man with us." * "The religion of the Jews, as taught by Moses, had presented for their worship a being of terrific character, cruel, vindictive, capricious and unjust." † With such deliberate blasphemy reason has nothing to do. An appeal is made to the Bible itself; the extracts on this page alone from the thousands in the Bible, set the question at rest.

57. The Divine origin of the Holy Scriptures is proved from their power and efficiency on the hearts conduct of men. "He that believeth hath the witness in himself." However unlearned, however ignorant, every child of grace knows his Bible to be true, and can tell you "Whereas I was blind, now I see." The infidel hears this with supreme contempt; the feelings of a few deluded enthusiasts are unworthy of his examination and regard. But it is not merely a few of whom we thus speak. Tens and hundreds of thousands, have in all ages given the same account; and amongst these are multitudes of superior learning and abilities, and of acknowleged integrity and sober judgment; and their professions have been followed by a correspondent change of the outward conduct, and a walk and conversation as becometh the gospel.

The effects of the Bible on human society are

---

* Jefferson's Mem. Vol. 4, pp. 271, let. 130.
† Jefferson's Mem. Vol. 4, pp. 326, let. 153.

equally evident. The spirit of its Divine precepts gives to society its firmest bond and cement. Here the marriage contract reposes on the principles of its first institution ; and women, unnaturally degraded in every heathen land, have been restored to their loved and honored place in the family. Are these the effects of a cunningly-devised fable? Or rather are not these things produced by the words of eternal life ?

The uncorrupted preservation of the books of the Old and New Testaments.

58. In general the facts and arguments already used to prove these books genuine and authentic, prove also their uncorrupted preservation. But more particularly the Hebrew Nation have in every age regarded their sacred books with peculiar reverence. Their own historians assert that no torments could induce them to change a single letter.* In our Saviour's time upon earth the nation was divided into various sects, yet we do not find that they charged each other with having corrupted their Scriptures. The Pentateuch contained their constitution and laws ; the book of Joshua recorded the division of their possessions, and designated the boundaries of the different tribes. In these books, forgery at first, or alteration afterwards, was impossible. The book of Psalms was in daily use in the temple worship ; the proverbs of Solomon were in every cottage, in every tent. While the temple worship continued, and the nation existed in Palestine, in these books no alteration could take place. In the historical records, the parts humbling to their national pride would have been first altered, if any alteration had been made ;

---

* Phi. a. lus. Ev. lib, 8, c. g, Jos. Con. Ap. lib. 1, § 8.

but these parts, and they are numerous, are still there.
The Samaritan Pentaituch, the Chaldaic paraphrase,
and the Greek translation, were each a separate guard
against alteration.   The prophets from Samuel to
Malachi were faithful reprovers of every sin ; yet
they say not a word of any corruption, either of the
historical, preceptive or prophetical books.   To all
these considerations may be added, what is indeed of
itself conclusive, that Jesus Christ and his apostles
never bring any such charge against the Jews, but
repeatedly refer to these books as the oracles of
God, consisting of the Law, the Prophets and the
Psalms, Luke xxiv, 25-27, 44-46 ; Rom. iii, 2.

59. Since the Christian era, the books of the Old
Testament have been appealed to and reverenced both
by Jews and Christians.   No alteration could have
been made by either without being detected by the
other.   The Greek translation had been made 265
years before that period ; it was read by those Jews
who understood Greek, and by such Greeks as chose
to read it, in every part of the Roman Empire.   In
the second century, if not in the first, these books
were translated into the Syriac and Latin, and in the
following centuries into various other languages.   The
Hebrew manuscripts, amounting to above eleven hundred in number, all agree with each other.   Under all
these circumstances, alteration by design was impracticable and impossible.   Mistakes in copying have
indeed taken place ; but a careful examination of the
different copies will always lead to true reading.
Thus we see :

1. That the Hebrew Scriptures were in the hands
of both Christians and Jews, and appealed to, and
reverenced, and guarded by each.

2. That a Greek translation existed in the days of the apostles, and that translations into other languages quickly followed.

3. That amongst the numerous manuscripts collected from all parts of the world, there is an agreement perfectly substantial. To these three considerations nothing further need be added to prove that the Old Testament has come down to us uncorrupted and unaltered.

60. As it respects the books of the New Testament, this branch of the subject has been in a great measure anticipated. The facts and arguments adduced (Nos. 14-27) to prove that the books of the New Testament are genuine and authentic, prove also that they have come down to us pure and uncorrupted. It will not be contended that any alteration in these books could take place during the lives of the writers; and no historical fact is better established, than that during their lives Christian churches were established at Jerusalem, Rome, Corinth, Ephesus, Damascus, Antioch, and many other cities in every part of the Roman Empire. In every church the public reading and exposition of the Holy Scriptures was a part of their stated worship. No alteration could take place without the knowledge and acquiescence of both teachers and people, and without consent on the part of all the churches. For their future hopes founded on their belief of the truth of these writings, the primitive Christians suffered the loss of all things, endured every species of persecution, and in thousands of instances, death itself. Under all these circumstances, to suppose that all these churches would themselves deliberately alter these writings, is impossible and absurd.

61. The hostility of the Jews was co-eval with the first rise of Christianity, and has continued to the present day. If any change had been made in the sacred books of the Christians, these bitter opponents, as well as their heathen adversaries, would soon have charged them with it. Various sects also soon made their appearance in the Christian Church; and various heresies existed from the days of the apostles. In all controversies with their different opponents, the Christian Church appealed to the Scriptures as to a perfect standard. With so many seeking occasion against them, with so many continually watching to do them hurt, with Jews, heathens and heretics on every side, alteration or corruption in the record was impossible.

62. Another satisfactory consideration arises from the agreement of all the manuscripts of the New Testament, which have come down to us. Mistakes in copying exist in great numbers; but in no one material article do these mistakes make any alteration. The worst manuscript extant would not pervert one doctrine, or destroy one moral precept. By a comparison of these manuscripts with each other these mistakes are discoverable, and scriptural criticism has already in most cases restored the true reading. The agreement of so many separate and independent witnesses from all parts of Asia, Africa and Europe, proves that the sacred pages have come down to us pure and unaltered.

63. The agreement of the various translations of the New Testament with each other, and with our present Greek text, shows to a demonstration that from the period when these translations were made, no change has taken place in the original record. The

Latin and Syriac translations were made in the second century, if not in the first, as many learned men believe, the Gothic, A.D. 400; the Egyptian, A.D. 500; the English, A.D. 700; the Persian, A.D. 900. These dates are placed at periods when all admit that these translations existed. As we descend towards our own time many others were made ; and in the year A.D. 1383, the art of printing placed the whole Bible beyond the reach of alteration either from mistake or design.

64. The quotations of the Christian fathers, as far as these quotations extend, afford clear and positive testimony to the uncorrupted purity of the books of the New Testament. Limiting this evidence to the verses actually quoted, a great part of the New Testament, as we now have it, is proved from this source alone. To notice this evidence in detail, would far exceed the limits assigned to this work ; and a simple reference to it is all that is here intended.

FAREWELL COUNSELS—MISSIONS TO EASTERN ASIA.

In the earlier years of the Presbyterian Missions it was a common usage for the Executive Committee, through its secretary, to give farewell instructions or counsels to new missionaries, when they were leaving for their fields of labour, if their journey was to be made by a sea voyage. Dr. Swift, secretary, made addresses of this kind; Mr. Lowrie, also; both repeatedly. These were of general interest, and were listened to by large congregations.

But with the change of travelling to steam navigation, most missionaries preferred to remain with their friends at home until the latest hour of departure; and farewell services were usually conducted by their pastor or neighbouring ministers. The elaborate addresses formerly made seemed to be seldom suited to the occasion. In some cases, however, either method answered a good purpose. It may be of interest to insert here the address of Mr. Lowrie at a public meeting in the Brick Church, New York City, when the Rev. John A. Mitchell, of Charleston, S. C., and the Rev. Professor Robert W. Orr and his wife, of Cannonsburgh, Penn., embarked for Singapore as missionaries to the Chinese, December 6, 1838.

BELOVED BRETHREN—It is a subject of peculiar interest to the Executive Committee of the Board of Foreign Missions of the General Assembly, that one of their first acts is to deliver instructions to the first missionaries to China sent out by the Presbyterian Church. If we take into view the immense number of the Chinese people ; their general intelligence ; the progress they have made in civilization ; the remarkable fact, that not only the whole empire, but four other adjoining nations, read one language ; and also, that this entire population are "without Christ, aliens from His Church, and strangers to the covenants of promise, having no hope, and without God in the world,"—the solemn duty of the Church to send them the gospel will appear in a strong light. In discharge of this duty, little, comparatively, has been done by any branch of the Church ; and by our beloved Zion, until now, nothing has been even attempted. We rejoice that, in the good providence of God, a mission from the Presbyterian Church to this great but perishing people is prepared to embark, to carry to them a knowledge of Redeeming Love. May we not indulge the hope that in future her zeal and resources will, in a measure, make up for our past indifference, and that you, dear brethren, will be followed by large numbers, continued and increasing from year to year, till the whole empire of China, and the nations reading her language, shall be made to rejoice in the knowledge of the Saviour ! This result is in the promise and in the purpose of God, and His power will bring it to pass. Our present efforts, and those of sister churches who have preceded us, and are now engaged in the same blessed work, may be considered feeble and unimportant ; but all these efforts are in accordance with the appointed means for this very end, and are in obedience to the command of our blessed Lord. This is His plan :—let

His churches and His missionaries see to it that they become neither weary nor discouraged in His work. *We* may not live to see the triumph of His cause among the heathen, for we have all neglected our duty in this great work; but the day is coming when the churches will come up to the requirements of the word of God, and then they will see and rejoice in the final triumph of the cause of Christ; when the hearts of His people will be filled with joy and gladness, to see the glory which will be to God in the highest, in the general knowledge of the Redeemer's name.

The first Protestant missionary to China was the Rev. Dr. Morrison, a name most deservedly dear to all the churches. He was sent out in 1807 by the London Missionary Society, and laboured faithfully, and, for a great part of the time, alone in preparing the way for future labourers, till his death. The labours of this great man, in translating the Bible into the Chinese language, have been duly appreciated by all, and especially by every missionary to China. In part of these labours he was ably assisted by Dr. Milne, who joined him in 1813; but his early death, in 1822, left Dr. Morrison once more alone; and his life was graciously spared till these great works were finished.

The London Missionary Societies have in this field at present six missionaries; the American Board of Commissioners for Foreign Missions, including Singapore, Java, Sumatra and Siam, seventeen; the Episcopal Church in the United States, three; the American Baptist Board, three; and the Church of England Missionary Society, one. The whole number from all these is thirty. How few the labourers in this great field ! Surely the time has fully come, when the churches should pray the Lord of the harvest to send forth labourers into His harvest : and not pray only, but also *do* the will of their Lord, in sending to this perishing people the blessings they themselves so richly enjoy.

The empire of China extends through twenty-one degrees of latitude, and twenty-six degrees of longitude. There is considerable difference in the estimates of the number of square miles by those writers who are supposed to be best acquainted with the subject. Taking the medium of their estimates, China proper may be set down as containing a million and a half, and the whole empire five millions of square miles. Supposing this to be the most correct estimate, it will be seen that this great empire is more than one-fourth larger than all Europe, and is more than five times the size of the twenty-six United States.

The number of the population is also a matter of much uncertainty, though all writers agree in stating it to be very large. The best evidence on this subject seems to be the enumeration of the Chinese themselves. Their census of 1793 gave a population of 307,000,000, and of 1812 of 360,000,000.

The government would be a pure despotism were it not for some limitations and restrictions imposed by custom on the emperor. He is considered the source of all power and honour ; is styled the Son of Heaven ; and is an object of worship throughout the whole empire. Constant efforts are made by the government to impress the people with the belief that all its principles are strictly patriarchal—taken from the model of a family, and conforming to it in all respects. The emperor is said to be the father of his whole people ; the same penalty is prescribed for offences against each, and the same mourning at the death of the emperor that there is at that of the father of a family.

The emperor is assisted by various Boards at Pekin, not unlike our heads of departments ; and, under their direction, each province has a governor, a judge and a collector ; and under these again are various orders of Mandarins, amounting in the whole empire to 14,000.

The standing army consists of 80,000 men, and there are 700,000 militia, who receive a pittance of pay. The navy, although numbering many vessels and boats, is quite inefficient, and often unable to subdue the pirates on the coast.

The penal code of China contains many excellent provisions, expressed with great clearness and appropriate brevity. It is far in advance of that of any other Eastern nation. Its defect is a too great minuteness in the attempt to regulate every circumstance in common life. The great evil is in the administration, affording another sad evidence, on a large scale, that without the knowledge of the Bible, the rights of the people, and truth and righteousness, are unknown.

The character of the Chinese is perhaps as favourable as that of any other civilized people who are without God, and without a knowledge of His Word. Though but a part of the population can read, the readers are in every part of the empire, and in this respect, education is general. They are noted for their industry, and for their business habits ; they are remarkable for their respect for the aged, and they possess a mild and peaceable disposition. But alas! here we must stop; and describe other traits of character truly painful. They care nothing for truth, and are full of deceit; their self-love and ignorance make them proud, haughty and conceited, and all but themselves are barbarians; infanticide of female children has long been extensively perpetrated among them; and that universal mark of heathenism, the degradation of woman, prevails throughout the whole empire. The female infant is despised as soon as she is born; she is called even then a hated thing; and through life the law, and all the maxims and writings of their atheistical sages, are against her.

The religion of China is a strange mixture of atheism and idolatry. Three sects exist there—the followers of Confucius, the Buddhists, and the Doctors of Reason.

Confucius was born 550 years before the Christian era. His writings are preserved with great care and veneration; in them are many excellent maxims, but the good is intermixed with many things of the most evil and pernicious tendency. He acknowledged that he knew nothing about the existence of the gods, and respecting them preserved silence. Con-foo-tze, his most distinguished disciple, affirms that sufficient knowledge was not possessed to say that the gods had any existence; but he saw no difficulty in omitting the subject altogether. This doctrine of Confucius is the established religion of the empire, and, although its foundation thus reposes on atheism, there is an expensive state worship, with many imposing forms. Sacrifices are offered at the public expense to heaven—to the emperor—the earth—sun—moon—sages and other objects. The images and objects of worship of the common people are without

number or description; and the annual expense of
their idol worship is estimated by Dr. Morrison at
200,000,000 of dollars.

Buddhism is another form of their worship, but
this sect is merely tolerated. Which are the most
numerous in China, the followers of Buddha or of Confucius is not known. But, if the adjacent countries
be taken into account, no form of heathenism is
so prevalent as Buddhism. At this day, more than
half the human family are led captive by this delu-
sion of Satan. In this system, atheism is a leading
feature. The god they acknowledge and worship is a
mere abstraction; he is said to exist in a state of
eternal repose, caring for nothing, and without any
mental exercises whatever. They believe not in the
creation of the world, but in a succession of worlds;
yet they profess to believe in a state of future rewards and punishments; but these truths are so
mixed up with their fables of the metempsychosis of
the soul from one body to another that all salutary
influence on the conduct is lost. Not one ray of the
true light shines upon them. The whole system
makes the mass of the people more submissive to
their wretched and abandoned priesthood. There it
begins, and there it ends.

The Doctors of Reason constitute the third sect.
They are silent as to the being of a God, the immortality of the soul, or a state of future rewards and
punishments. They are given to magic and alchemy,
and spend much of their time and thoughts in pursuit of the elixir of life. They are also called Taouists.

Among the great mass of the people, these three
sects are not very distinctly marked; and many of
the superstitions of each are attended to by all. It

would indeed be difficult to describe the darkness, confusion, and obscurity of their practice and belief.

From this brief but melancholy survey of this great empire may be seen how greatly it needs the knowledge of the true God, and the way of salvation through Jesus Christ. The millions of China are perishing, and their dark and hopeless state calls most earnestly on the churches for relief. In responding to this call, and in devoting your lives to their benefit, it is proper for you, dear brethren, as well as for the Board under whose direction you go, and the churches whose missionaries you are, to know the difficulties which will meet your efforts to carry the gospel to them. It is, indeed, but an abstract of these difficulties that can be presented here ; and you will meet with others, unknown at present to us all.

1. The stern prejudices, and determined hostility, manifested of late by the Chinese government against the introduction of the gospel into China, present an obstacle to all benevolent efforts in behalf of this great people. These efforts must at present be made at a distance, and of course under disadvantages. But this obstacle, in the present state of Protestant missions, has been greatly overrated. The superabundant population of China, overflowing the limits of their native land, and finding resting-places in the neighbouring countries and islands, afford many opening fields for the churches to occupy, and where they may prepare and qualify their missionaries to be in readiness when God, in His providence, removes the principal barriers. In the meantime all the brethren sent out will be on missionary ground, labouring among the hundreds of thousands of Chinese who are

now perfectly accessible to their appropriate labours. Were every barrier now removed, few more facilities would exist for learning the language; for providing and conducting suitable schools and higher semina- ries; for raising up and instructing a native ministry; for translating the Scriptures and preparing other suitable books; and, in general, for using the mighty agency of the press, than are now to be found.

2. Another discouraging circumstance is, that the labourers are so few. Few, indeed, they are for so great a work! But let not this discourage our efforts; rather let it increase them. The number is increasing from year to year; the evangelical churches are be- coming awake to the importance of this great work; and, above all, the Lord of the harvest, in answer to the prayers of His people, will send forth "labourers into His harvest."

3. Another obstacle is the advanced position occu- pied by the Church of Rome on the borders of the empire, and, to some extent, even within its limits. The whole of the Phillipine Islands, as well as Macao, is under her control; and to the importance of this subject she is quite awake, and in a great measure prepared with able men and abundant means to send into the interior her adulterated form of the Christian faith. Instead of discouraging this state of things ought to engage the true churches to redoubled efforts. Although the influence of this false religion exists strongly in this field, it exists also in most other fields, and it must be met by the Church of Christ, let it exist where it may. This influence is indeed pernicious, but its days are numbered, and it will come to an end at the brightness of the coming of the Lord.

4. When you come to teach the Chinese themselves, you will find their minds preoccupied by the most contradictory and the most confused and absurd notions of their own superstitions. You will find atheism and idolatry existing in the same mind. If you speak to them of God, they will point to the visible heavens; for thus their books teach them. The providence of God is unknown to them; and they will tell you that the heavens, earth and the sages, are united in the government of the world. If you speak to them of virtue and vice, of sin and holiness, you will find their views most indefinite and obscure. These and many other things equally painful, and which for a long series of generations have become, as it were, part of their existence, will require of you unremitting perseverance, faith and prayer, lest you faint and grow weary in your work.

5. Their great veneration for their sages will meet you as an obstacle at every step. They praise Confucius in language similar to what we use in the praise of God, our Maker. When you speak to them of a *crucified* Saviour, to whom their emperors and their sages are required to be in subjection, they turn from the instruction with contempt and loathing. "It is foolishness unto them," and so they literally call it.

They are taught from infancy, and from age to age, to think themselves superior to all other people. Confucius and his disciples have in their writings strongly inculcated this feeling; it has become with them a second nature, interwoven with all their thoughts, and incorporated with their very language; and the government has at all times, for political purposes, nourished and cherished it in all their transactions with foreigners, and in every state paper relating to them.

7. Much labour will be required in fully learning the singular and difficult language of this people. It is true, this has heretofore been greatly overrated; but it will still be found to require long and patient application, to obtain a perfect knowledge of it. To master this language fully, however, is an object of so much importance, that the Executive Committee earnestly call your attention to this subject. What is even at this time most wanted is a translation of the Bible into Chinese, which, while it faithfully preserves the spirit of the original, will use such expressions and national idioms as are familiar, and, as far as mere language is concerned, will be acceptable to the people of China. The translation made by Morrison and Milne has been found by succeeding missionaries to be deficient in the use of such modes of expression as are in use in the Chinese writings. By some of the missionaries now in the field a new translation was some time ago commenced, of which the New Testament has been finished and printed. Other missionaries, however, while they admit that defects exist in the former translation, have made objections to this, as going to the other extreme, and in some places giving not a translation, but a paraphrase of the original, by the use of the Chinese idioms. The subject is one of acknowledged difficulty, owing to the peculiar structure of the Chinese language, and the great number of idioms in it peculiar to itself; but it lies at the foundation of all our efforts in behalf of China; and hence the necessity of a perfect knowledge of the language. Let these considerations stimulate and encourage you

in your efforts to attain this object. By these means you may have the honour, in connection with missionaries from sister churches, of producing a translation that will be to China what our present translation is to us.

We have thus brought to your view some of the difficulties that you will have to meet in your field of labour. But, in view of these and of all others, of whatever kind, we say to you, dear brethren, be not discouraged. To this great work you go not forth alone. You know who it is that hath said, "Lo, I am with you always, even unto the end of the world." Keep constantly in mind what God requires you to do, and what it is that He has reserved to do Himself. Your duty is clear, and, in humble dependence on His grace, be faithful in the discharge of it. What more can you want than the promise of the Saviour's presence? What more can you possibly receive than His company with you always? If we could add anything to this for your encouragement, we would remind you that the glory of the Redeemer is here concerned. The millions of China are promised to Him; the day is coming when in all her valleys and on all her mountains, His name will be known and with sweetest sound dwell on every tongue; and the means which God has appointed to bring about this glorious result, is the performance of those duties in which you, and those who send you forth, are called upon to engage. Nothing can be more certain than that these efforts are in obedience to the Saviour's commands; that this is His plan for the extension of His kingdom; that He is with His servants always, even unto the end; that His glory will be promoted by the heathen being brought into His fold; and, finally, that this is His work, and He will bring it to pass. Let these truths cheer you in your darkest hours. Your trials may be severe, as you go in advance of others, and your lives may be spent more in preparatory, than in direct efforts for the heathen; but even this will not change the nature of the work itself, for this part of the work must first be done; and what is accomplished by you will prepare the way for others.

Until you shall have reached your field of labour, and have made the examinations suggested in the letter of instructions you have already received, the ultimate location of the mission cannot be decided on. At Singapore you will find a temporary resting-place, affording you many facilities for learning the language, and prosecuting the inquiries with which you have been charged. In the permanent location of the mission, care must be taken not to interfere with any existing Protestant Mission; and that there be such numbers of Chinese in the vicinity as will require not only your labours, but also those of some of the other brethren who may follow you.

And now, in conclusion, dear brethren, let us affectionately exhort you to take care of your own souls. This admonition we would also take to ourselves. If the Apostle to the Gentiles found it necessary to be watchful and to take all care, lest, when he preached the gospel to others, he himself should be a castaway, how much more is it necessary for each of us, who are so far behind him in conformity to the holy image of our Lord, to examine carefully what spirit we are of. "Not every one that saith unto me, Lord, Lord, shall enter into the kingdom of heaven, but he that doeth the will of my Father which is in heaven." Without His love in our hearts, though we speak with the tongues of men and of angels, we are but as sounding brass or a tinkling cymbal. We may have the gift of prophecy, and understand mysteries and all knowledge, and still be nothing. We may bestow our goods on charitable objects; we may endure the hardships and privations of a missionary life, at home or abroad, we may even give our bodies to be burned, but unless our motives and our hearts are sanctified by the grace of God it will profit us nothing. "Let us take heed then, brethren, lest there be in any of us an evil heart of unbelief in departing from the living God." But whilst it is our sacred duty to take heed to these solemn warnings in the Word of God, the example of the same apostle affords us the most assured encouragement, and in his experience we see the fruits of a holy life when he came to die. Before he left the earth he speaks to us as from the vestibule of heaven, "I have fought a good fight, I have finished my course, I have kept the faith : henceforth there is laid up for me a crown of righteousness, which the Lord, the righteous Judge, shall give me at that day ; and not to me only, but unto all them also that love His appearing."

You are sent by the churches to make known the riches of a Saviour's love to the perishing heathen. But, whilst you point them to the "Lamb of God which taketh away the sins of the world," remember, beloved brethren, that He is your Saviour ; also that to Him you must look for assistance, whilst engaged in His service here ; and that on Him rests your own hopes beyond the grave. Let your reliance on Him be simple and entire ; and fear not to trust yourselves wholly to Him in life and in death. Take Him with you in the ship; the great expanse of waters over which you are called to pass are His; and all the storms and dangers of the mighty deep are under His control. In your labours among the heathen stand near the cross, and look to God in constant, earnest prayer, for the blessing of the Holy Ghost, whose work it is to apply to the soul the redemption purchased by Christ. When all your labours are done, and you are called to pass through the valley of the shadow of death, fear not to trust the Saviour then. He will meet you in that hour, and after death you will still be where He reigns and controls all things; "Seeing then that we have a great High Priest that is passed into the heavens, Jesus, the Son of God, let us hold fast our profession. For we have not a high priest which cannot be touched with the feeling of our infirmities; but was in all points tempted like as we are, yet without sin. Let us therefore come boldly to the throne of grace, that we may obtain mercy, and find grace to help in time of need." Finally, brethren, *farewell.* Be perfect, be of good comfort, be of one mind; live in peace! and the God of love and peace shall be with you. Amen.

THE Rev. Robert W. Sawyer and wife embarked for Western Africa, October 6, 1841. The usual instructions were addressed to them by Mr. Lowrie, secretary, in behalf of the Board:

DEAR FRIENDS. The work of a minister of Jesus Christ is the most momentous in which a human being can engage. The best qualified may exclaim with the apostle, "Who is sufficient for these things?" In every field of labour Divine assistance is needed; and especially so, when the call of God is to labour in the dark places of the earth, far away from the sustaining influences of the churches of the living God, and the company and fellowship of his ministers and people. You, dear brother, have just been ordained, by the proper judicatory of the church, acting in the Saviour's name and by his authority. You have been designated also by the agents of the church, to go far hence unto the Gentiles, to speak unto them that they may be saved; to call them away from their senseless idolatry, and to tell them of the only true God, and of the love of Jesus, and point them to Him as the Lamb of God that taketh away the sin of the world.

One of the first sacrifices you are called to make is to part from your friends and relatives, from father and mother, from brothers and sisters, from those in whose company you have lived so long, that their endeared society has, in a manner, become a part of your existence. This trial is so severe, so painful to flesh and blood, so desolating to the natural feelings of the heart, that many of God's professing people are unwilling to meet it. They cannot give up a beloved son, they cannot thus part for life with a beloved daughter. But the cause of Christ requires this sacrifice, severe and painful as it is; and when the Saviour's glory is concerned, and the eternal interests of perishing men, these light afflictions which are but for a moment ought not to be even named.

By your own free choice, and with the approbation and sanction of the Executive Committee, Western Africa has been selected as the field of your future labours. A beloved brother has just fallen in that field, and you have been appointed to supply his place. This circumstance throws a more than ordinary degree of solemnity over our present meeting. It is a serious thing to be thus baptised for the dead. But may we not hope that in as much as your appointment has been made, after much prayer to God for his direction, it will meet with his approbation.

Every field of missionary labour has obstacles to the efforts of the church and discouragements peculiar to itself. In some "the man of sin opposeth and exalteth himself above all that is called God or is worshipped; so that He as God sitteth in the temple of God, shewing himself that He is God." In others, the exterminating spirit of the false prophet suspends the sword over every one that turns to the light. Others, again, are prevented by an ignorant despotism from hearing the truth; and, in others, is the influence of unhealthy climates. This last is the case with Western Africa; and this obstacle is a serious one. Every branch of the Church which has engaged in missionary labours there, has found it so. In deciding, therefore, on what is duty, we are called to examine the subject in the light of God's word, and of His providence; and above all, to look to Him for wisdom and direction.

The first question to be examined is, shall this field be abandoned, the missionaries now there withdrawn, and the benighted inhabisants, excluded from the efforts of the Church, be left to perish in ignorance and sin?

Let it be admitted, that to plant the Church in Africa, will cause the death of some of God's servants. If we take the example of the apostles for our guidance, we will not find in this a sufficient reason for leaving the millions in this country in the unmolested possession of Satan. It cost Stephen and James their lives to witness for the Saviour at Jerusalem; and Paul was "ready not to be bound only, but also to die at Jerusalem for the name of the Lord Jesus." In view of the bonds and afflictions which everywhere waited for him, he could say, "But none of these things move me, neither count I my life dear unto myfelf, so that I might finish my course with joy, and the ministry which I have received of the Lord Jesus, to testify the gospel of the grace of God." It were easy to multiply examples of the sufferings of the apostles and first Christians, in their labours to build up the church. In no instance did the fear of death deter them from preaching the glorious gospel of the Son of God. They were influenced by His Spirit, and acted in view of His high and holy example. "Hereby perceive we the love of God, because he laid down

His life for us; and we ought to lay down our lives for the brethren."

There is a tendency in some minds to draw an inference against the missionary work from the death of a missionary, which is not thought of in the death of a minister among the churches at home. But this position will not bear examination. Within a few months, how large has been the number of beloved brethren, most of them in the prime of life, who have been called home from their labours; yet no one infers from these dispensations of Divine providence, that it is not the duty of the church to use every means to supply their places. Nay, all agree, that for this purpose, increased efforts, and increased prayer to the Lord of the harvest, together with a deeper humility and repentance for her unfaithfulness become the special duty of the church in these seasons of rebuke and affliction. These principles apply in all their force to the death of our dear brethren in the foreign field; and the church is not at liberty to apply one rule of duty in regard to her ministers at home, and another rule to her ministers abroad. The word of God makes no such distinction, the field for her agency is the world. Although there be a risk to human life, in sending to benighted Africa the knowledge of the Saviour, his commission, the spirit that was in Him, and the example of His apostles require it to be done. In thus engaging in the Lord's work, the Church is not making experiments; she is but obeying the command of the Saviour; and if she persevere in carrying out His commission, her success is just as certain as that her Redeemer rose from the dead. The redemption of Ethiopia, and her inbringing to the fold of Christ are in the purpose of God; and her very name is mentioned in His glorious promise. "Ethiopia shall soon stretch out her hands to God." Ps. lxvii. 31. Now the word of God is explicit, that His purposes of love and mercy, and all His promises shall be fulfilled by the use of the appointed means. By the preaching of the gospel all nations shall be brought to the knowledge of the Saviour; and Africa, though long oppressed and trampled under foot, with her benighted and degraded people, shall, by the blessing of God, on this, His appointed agency, be brought to the light and liberty of the children of God.

As the constitution of coloured men can endure the climate of Africa better than white men, the question may be asked, Why not commit the entire work to them? The answer to this is, that we have not got suitable and qualified men of this class to take the charge of this important work. If it be left to them, the efforts to bless this benighted people must for the present be postponed. Hence the absolute necessity of educated and qualified white men.

But although the agency of white men cannot at first be dispensed with, it is not required that the whole missionary work be done by them. On the contrary, there is so much that from the first can be done by qualified assistants, that even with an equal number of them the force of the mission would be doubled. Hence it is the part of wisdom to employ the agency of coloured men, as far as their qualifications will permit. At present, teachers and assistants of this class can be obtained; others of higher attainments, men of piety and zeal for this great work, will in time be prepared, both in this country and among the natives, to take the burden of the missionary

work in Africa on themselves ; so that the blessings
of the gospel will be carried to this benighted land
chiefly by the agency of her own children.

The whole of the Western coast, from Sierra
Leone to the Sinoe River, had long been the mart of
the slave trade. First the British, and then the
American colonies arrested its progress on large sections of the coast ; but it was only within the last
year that the slave factories at the Gallinos and New
Cess were broken up. The whole country back of
these colonies has been the seat of this murderous
traffic, which to a large extent still continues. The
part of the coast lying between the Sinoe River and
Cape Palmas, and occupied by the Kroos, the Grand
Sesters, and the Grebos, has, for the most part,
escaped this dreadful scourge. No missionary has
ever resided among the Kroos, or the Grand Sesters
on the coast, or any of the tribes behind them. The
first station for the mission must, from the state of
the country, be on the coast. Every tribe in that
region is most anxious to have missionaries to reside
among them.

The Kroos living on the coast claim to be first
supplied before they will permit a station among
their neighbors more inland, who are equally de-
sirous of missionaries with themselves. In a short
time we hope to have another station, on the highlands in the Waw country, leaving the station on the
coast in the charge of the coloured members of the
mission. This point gained, we have good reason to
believe that the health of our brethren will not suffer
materially from the climate in the interior ; and that
we may then look forward to the permanent continuance of the mission without more than ordinary risk

to the health and life of the brethren sent from among ourselves.

By our last accounts from Africa, the mission family now there had passed safely through the first attack of fever, which is always the most dangerous, and which, in this instance, proved fatal to one of the brethren. The vessel that takes you out, carries also a house prepared to be set up, and large enough to accommodate two families. The vessel will touch at Cape Palmas, and it is arranged, that Mr. Canfield will proceed to the Kroo country, taking assistants with him to set up the house when the materials are landed. A boat will also be sent with you sufficiently large to run between the station and either of the colonies. It will most likely be best for you to remain at Cape Palmas until the building at Settra Kroo is ready to receive you, or even longer, if that be deemed best by yourself and the brethren there.

Whilst it is the duty of the church, and of all her judicatories and her Board of Foreign Missions, as well as of all her missionaries, while labouring for the spread of the gospel, to mature the best plans for carrying forward the work, it is equally the duty of all to contemplate with awe and reverence, and with deep humility, the Divine sovereignty, and to acknowledge in all things the overruling providence of God. Without His approval every plan and counsel, however wise to human view, will be turned to foolishness and disappointment. It becomes us, then, to look to the word of God for direction, and to follow the example of His servants as therein recorded for our instruction. It is worthy of our imitation how frequently the apostle to the Gentiles, though commissioned by the Saviour himself, and living for

His glory, and labouring more abundantly than all others, refers, in all his plans and purposes, to the will of the Lord. "I must by all means keep this feast that cometh in Jerusalem; but I will return again to you, if God will." Acts xviii. 21. "Making request, if by any means now at length I might have a prosperous journey, by the will of God to come unto you." Rom. i. 10. "That I may come unto you with joy, by the will of God, and may with you be refreshed." Rom. xv. 32. "But I will come to you shortly, if the Lord will." 1 Cor. iv. 19. "For I will not see you now by the way; but I trust to tarry a while with you, if the Lord permit." I. Cor. xvi. 7. "And this will we do, if God permit." Heb. vi. 3.

Such also was the practice of the prophets. "And the king said unto Zadoc, carry back the ark of God into the city; if I shall find favour in the eyes of the Lord, He will bring me again and shew me both it and its habitation. But if He thus say, I have no delight in thee; behold, here am I, let Him do to me as seemeth good to him." 2 Sam. xv. 25–26.

"Then I proclaimed a fast there at the river Ahava, that we might afflict ourselves before our God, to seek of Him a right way for us, and for our little ones; and for all our substance. For I was ashamed to require of the king a band of soldiers and horsemen to help us against the enemy in the way; because we had spoken unto the king, saying, The hand of our God is upon all them for good that seek Him; but His power and His wrath is against all them that forsake Him. So we fasted and besought our God for this; and He was entreated of us." Ezra viii. 21–23.

"Who is he that saith and it cometh to pass when the the Lord commandeth it not." Lam. iii. 37.

"And all the inhabitants of the earth are reputed as nothing, and He doeth according to His will in the army of heaven, and among the inhabitants of the earth ; and none can stay His hand or say unto Him, What doest Thou ?" Dan. iv. 35. In everything we do, therefore, in the Saviour's service, it becomes us to act under the influence of these solemn truths, and in all our proposed measures, follow the example of the prophets and apostles, saying, *If the Lord will.*

In contemplating your field of labour, whilst we would not disguise from you, nor from ourselves, that it is of more than ordinary peril to life and health, still it is not required that you go there with the spirit of a martyr ; but with the spirit of a missionary of the cross, whose wish and desire is to labour in the Saviour's cause, as long as the Saviour sees good to prolong your life and health. If there be danger in this field, there is also great need of labourers. Generation after generation of immortal beings are there living and dying under the cruel dominion of Satan. There is a people for whom every thing remains to be done, a people who have had a double portion of the wormwood and the gall.

Let us pause a moment to consider and weep over the complications of evil and oppression which trample this people in the dust. First, the blasting influence of the slave trade, extending over a great part of the western coast, breaking up every bond of society, arraying the different communities against each other, and making it the interest of every man to quarrel with his neighbour, that he may betray and sell him to the man-stealer and the pirate. Next the despotism and oppression of their rulers, by which almost the whole community are reduced to slavery, and subjected to the caprice, avarice and cruelty of those who ought to protect and cherish them. Then comes their miserable and unprincipled priesthood, their fetish men, their witch-finders, their devil-men, their rain-makers, with all their train of debasing and cruel forms of worship, and low unmeaning idolatry. We turn to the darker shades of the picture, and there we find poor, degraded woman. No plague spot so deep as this. Here is half the community, the mothers of the rising generation, brutalized, and doomed to the most abject depression, where all are depressed and wretched. But the darkest shade still remains to be considered, and that is the closing scene. To them no ray of light breaks across the thick darkness that rests upon the grave. Death is to them a most dreaded and most dreadful enemy, and from his approach they shrink with terror and despair to the last. Nor is this to be wondered at, for he comes to them in unknown terrors. The love of a dying Saviour has never reached their ears; the message of mercy, of pardon for sin, of peace with God, has never been sent to them. They have lived in the region and shadow of death, and they die surrounded with terror and remorse, with every prospect shrouded in the darkness of the tomb. O, how much this people need the knowledge of that remedy which has the promise of this life and that which is to come. How emphatically to them would the message of the gospel be good-tidings of great joy!

And now, dear brother and sister, the providence of God has opened the way for you to engage in the great work which brought the Saviour to our world.

No privations or sufferings of His followers can equal His while fulfilling His Divine mission. The trials you may be called to endure, cannot be compared with His in the garden of Gethsemane, when His sweat was as it were great drops of blood falling down to the ground. Should you even be called to an early death, it will not compare with His on the cross, and His contest there with the powers of darkness. You may indeed be called "to fill up that which is behind of the afflictions of Christ, in your flesh for His body's sake, which is the Church;" but even then, you have His blessed promise, that "he will never leave you nor forsake you." You will find it profitable, and so will all His followers, to review and meditate upon the terms of discipleship, as laid down by our Lord Himself. "The disciple is not above his master, nor the servant above his lord. It is enough for the disciple to be as his master, and the servant to be as his lord. He that findeth his life shall lose it; and he that loseth his life for my sake shall find it. He that loveth father or mother more than me is not worthy of me; and he that loveth son or daughter more than me is not worthy of me. He that taketh not up his cross and followeth not after me, is not worthy of me. If any man will come after me, let him deny himself, and take up his cross daily and follow me."

Just as you live under the influence of these requirements, will you find the sustaining presence of the Saviour. Should it be the will of God that your constitution can bear the climate to which you go, there never was a brighter prospect of usefulness than is now before you. Dark and waste and dreary as are the moral desolations of the people to whom you are sent, there is not, perhaps, anywhere a more interesting field of missionary labour; and as far as the inhabitants are concerned, one that is more encouraging. They are found to be of a teachable disposition, and many of them affectionate and confiding; and when brought to the knowledge of the truth, consistent and orderly professors of the name of Christ. Among the tribes on the coast, and those immediately inland, there is a great field of labour and much work to be done; but our Master's vineyard lies also beyond all these, stretching far into the interior, and indeed embracing every tribe and people, whether wandering in the deserts, dwelling in cities, or solitary places, in the bosom of the forests, or on the banks of the lakes and rivers. All these are included in the command of the Saviour to the Church, and all these are included in his purposes of love and mercy. The way is fully open to commence the missionary work among them; and the progress of the truth from tribe to tribe, will still further and further prepare the way of the Lord, till the good news shall reach the most remote and obscure corner of the land.

Go forward, then, dear friends, without despondency. Present duty is our concern, and results belong to God. Live near the blessed Saviour. "Let your loins be girded about, and your lights burning; and ye yourselves like unto men that wait for their Lord." In the prayers of God's people we trust you will not be forgotten; and whilst in the name of the Church we bid you God speed, whilst we say farewell, we would with adoring reverence commend you to the care and keeping of the living God; and may his grace, mercy and peace be with you! Amen.

THE WORK OF FOREIGN MISSIONS.

THE MISSIONARY SECRETARYSHIP.

Prior to Mr. Lowrie's official connection with the cause of missions, his attention had been called to this subject, not only by his own study of the Sacred Scriptures and his acquaintance with missionary information in general, but by what may be called special orderings of Providence. One of these was that one of his brothers-in-law had been led to go as a lay missionary to an Indian tribe, but there soon lost his health and returned to his friends. For the sake of medical aid he came to the town of Butler, and soon after died in his brother-in-law's house. The second was his practical knowledge of African questions, in our country and in Africa, acquired in Washington. He became acquainted also with missionaries to western Africa—Messrs. Pinney, Cloud, and Laird, the first missionaries to Liberia—a noble company. The third, beginning in 1830–31, when his eldest son consulted his father and mother, as to the great question to him, whether he ought to go as a missionary?

The brief remarks made at the farewell meeting in Philadelphia, 1833, and later matters, probably directed the attention of many persons in the churches to Mr. Lowrie as a corresponding secretary of the Western Foreign Missionary Society, of the Synod of

Pittsburg, in 1835, to succeed the first secretary, the Rev. Dr. E. P. Swift, in the event of his resignation. This appointment was afterwards made, but he felt constrained to decline it. A year later, in August, 1836, when this appointment was urgently renewed, it appeared to be his duty to accept it—with the understanding that he should enter upon its duties when his official engagements in Washington could be closed.

In a secular point of view this change would hardly be considered an enviable one. The office in Washington was then regarded as one of the most desirable in the federal city,—in its sufficient salary, its personal associations, and its not being subject to political changes. A few years later it was understood, in a limited circle, that the office of Secretary of the Treasury of the United States was at his option. If so, it must have been on full acquaintance, as the President had known him for several years. They had been in the senate together, and a part of the time also members of the Standing Committee of Finance. But the decision had been made. And over thirty years of longer life confirmed the conviction that the missionary secretaryship had been appointed from on high. Its opportunities of serving our Saviour in the promotion of His cause were rightly appreciated.

This office was accepted, however, at a time of great perplexity. Serious controversies existed between the old and the new school parts of the Presbyterian Church, tending to the separation, which afterwards occurred. The cause of foreign missions was not much affected at first by these dissensions; but for a time it was feared that great evils would result from extreme measures. Mr. Lowrie was in sympathy with the views commonly taken of controverted questions in western Pennsylvania, where but little mere party feeling existed on church questions; but where the Western Foreign Missionary Society was awakening much interest in the cause of foreign missions, in which he felt the deepest concern. The scriptural principle, that the work of missions at home and abroad appertains to *the organized church*, and not chiefly nor incidentally to voluntary societies, was recognized by the first general assembly, in 1789, and by synods and presbyteries long before that time. This principle was not held by all in later days; but it is now recognized by the reunited church, and it is remarkably verified in the great enlargement of its foreign missions.

In the choice of the Secretary of Foreign Missions, the Synodical Society was greatly favored by Divine Providence as to its first incumbent, the Rev. E. P. Swift, D. D.;* and also in its second appointment, the Hon. Walter Lowrie, succeeding Dr. Swift. Of the General Assembly's Board, he became the first secretary. In both cases it was of great moment that the right men should be appointed, possessing eminent ability, earnest consecration, large experience, and the full confidence of the Church. Such a minister was Dr. Swift; such an elder was Mr. Lowrie. The former, by his eminent gifts and grace, was earnestly sought again for the pulpit, after the new society had been well begun. The latter, by his varied gifts in business lines, by a deep religious experience, and by his standing in the churches, was evidently called to the great work of his life, lasting

---

* See Dr. Ashbel Green's History, pp. 106–110.

until old age, after thirty years of missionary service. How different would have been their record if they had been different men—men of younger years, for example, of less judgment, of less sterling common sense, of less industry, and especially of less devoted piety.

YEARS OF SPECIAL INTEREST.

The years 1835–1837 were years of special interest in the Foreign Missions of the Presbyterian Church. The Western Foreign Missionary Society had consented to its being transferred to the General Assembly in 1835. The refusal of the General Assembly, by a close vote, to accept this transfer in 1836, led the society to resume its charge of the missions, after serious inconvenience. But these painful events were overruled by Divine Providence and by the influence of the Holy Spirit, so as to promote a deeper interest in the cause of missions, in conducting its organized work as a Church.

Accordingly the General Assembly of 1837 was led to organize its Board of Foreign Missions. By this Board the missions of the Society were cordially accepted, including its valuable property free from any encumbrance,—with its income, and all its interests. All were accepted in the same year by the Board, with due legal forms. The missionaries thus transferred to the Board had been sent to certain Indian tribes, Western Africa, North India, and partly commenced in Siam and China. A goodly number of missionaries had been sent forth. Among them five devoted labourers—three ministers and two married ladies—had been called to their rest in heaven.

The income of the Society had increased each year,

from $5,331.60, May 1st, 1833, to $33,560.26, May 1st, 1838. Its bequests in the same period from $100.00 to $1,034.88. The balance then on hand and made over to the Board, beginning its income, was $3,107. It is remarkable that the receipts of the Society's last year, so far as ascertained, exceeded the amount given to foreign missions in the same year by all other agencies, old and new, of the Presbyterian body. The time had come for testing more fully the principle and the plan of Church work in missions.

OFFICES OF THE BOARD REMOVED TO NEW YORK.

The practical work of changing the headquarters of the missions was facilitated by a recent measure of the W. F. M. Society of Pittsburgh—its organizing certain "Boards of Agency" in leading cities—Baltimore, Louisville, Indianapolis, Cincinnati, Philadelphia, and New York. The Board of Agency in New York was effectively organized, and would probably have become the General Board of the Old School part of the Church, if difficulties had continued in the General Assembly. The Agency Boards answered good purposes, in promoting interest in the cause of missions, but were discontinued when the G. A. Board was organized by the Assembly, and transferred to an eastern city. In New York the Agency Board held its session in the Chapel of the First Presbyterian Church, in Wall street, in the Brick Church, or in Cedar street and Duane street Lecture Rooms—from time to time. Eminent ministers and elders were appointed on these agencies.

When the Board of the General Assembly was removed to New York, its first meeting was held in the Wall street chapel. It rented for its office the one-half of a somewhat large room in the Brick Church chapel, fronting on the City Hall Park. The other half being occupied by the N. Y. Colonization Society. This half room was entirely inadequate. A third story of No. 247 Broadway, opposite the park, was then rented; but in the absence of "elevators" was found to be inconvenient, particularly as to freight for shipment to the missions. Rooms in City Hall Place, near the park, were then obtained; but lacked both space and light for the growing work of the Board. Most grateful to all, occupants and visitors, was the Mission House, 23 Centre street, still near the park. This good building was erected in 1842, at a cost of nearly $22,000—contributed chiefly by friends in New York, but also in many parts of the country. It sold some years afterwards for $75,000. Its site had become unsuitable. It had the great merits of being "down town," near the Post Office, Custom House, shipping and other business houses, and easily accessible from near and far.

In this location the Board followed the example of some of the leading Missionary Boards in London, which are near the Bank of England. When New York includes Brooklyn and other municipalities, and becomes the "Greater New York," the question may arise whether the Board should not remove its offices again to the vicinity of the City Hall Park. And then it may be wise to occupy exclusively, as formerly, a smaller building.

Looking forward still further, to a re-united Church, and to a still growing West, including the Pacific States, it may become expedient to organize two or three Foreign Mission Boards, with proper reference to the existing Providential circumstances, and to due economy in expense, as well as to the efficient conduct of the Missions.

VISIT TO SOUTHERN CHURCHES.

In the early circumstances of the Board, it was considered expedient for the secretary to spend several winter months of 1842 on a visit to churches in the Southern States. He was everywhere received with a cordial welcome, and with good results to the missionary cause. One case of special interest occurred about this period, which made him temporarily a slaveholder. A liberal gentleman in New Orleans had decided to give all his slaves their liberty. They were about a hundred in number. There were legal difficulties to be overcome. Besides, this gentleman felt the importance of their being prepared for liberty and self-support. He was already taking steps in this direction, having selected two of the young men to be educated at his charge, one as a teacher, the other as a doctor, at some college in the North, if this were practicable. His acquaintance with Mr. Lowrie, when he was in New Orleans, and the knowledge of his public life in Washington, led to his conferring with him on the subject which he had so much at heart. It was settled that the two young men should be sent to him without change in their legal condition, and then he should obtain for them the kindly charge of their education at some good college, after his giving them their freedom, being furnished with suitable credentials for this purpose. These measures were accomplished. The slaves received their freedom; the young men their education; unhappily not as complete as was hoped for, owing to their lack of energy.

On this southern journey, in a severe winter, owing to unavoidable exposure in those days, not a little danger to health was incurred. On a part of the way he had been accompanied by Mrs. Lowrie, his second wife, Miss Mary K. Childs, with whom he had become acquainted in Washington. She now made an extended visit to her married brother's family, Mr. Otis Childs, of Springfield, Mass., living in Georgia. She earnestly sympathized with her husband in his devotion to the cause of missions; and greatly endeared herself to his family, as well as to the numerous missionaries who for many years accepted their hospitality.

MISSION FUNDS FAITHFULLY APPLIED.

In the Annual Report of 1842, page 26, a clear and valuable statement is made to show how the Board secures complete responsibility in the expenditure of all moneys entrusted by the churches to its charge. After stating on pages 24 and 25 the various objects in the work of missions for which pecuniary means are indispensable, the Report proceeds :

"Here it may not be improper to notice an aspect of the Foreign Missionary cause connected with the foregoing remarks. What assurance, it may be asked, have those who make these contributions that they will be faithfully applied? What responsibility exists for the proper disbursement of large sums, in places so distant, and by so many individuals? These questions are pertinent and important, and ought to be distinctly and fully answered. This will best be accomplished by a simple exposition of the course now employed.

"All donations by churches, societies, and individuals, are charged to the Treasurer on the books of the office, and published in the Missionary Chronicle ; and no money is paid but on appropriations made by the Executive Committee.

"The expenses at home are kept under distinct heads, and published in the report of the Treasurer at the end of the year.

"For the missions abroad detailed estimates, made out carefully by the missionaries, in view of their wants and circumstances, are sent home in advance, which are approved or modified by the Committee, according to the prospect of receipts for the coming year. By these estimates the wants and prospects of all the missions are brought before them ; and it is an important part of their duty to dispose of them to the best advantage. It ought to be here noted, that every mission, and every proposed enlargement, pass every year under the supervision and control of the Board and the General Assembly, thus leaving to the Committee but the details of the work. When the estimates are returned, the missionaries know the amount they may expect to receive during the year, unless the receipts enable the Committee to forward additional sums, where they are wanted.

"Every remittance made is charged to the Treasurer of each mission respectively, on the books of the office ; and a detailed statement of the expenditures, at stated periods, properly examined and certified by the whole mission, is sent to the office. It is then examined by the Committee, and entered on the books of the Treasurer. If any item requires explanation, which rarely occurs, it is immediately asked for.

"By this procedure the whole amount received is

accounted for. The whole expenditure, with all its details, is recorded, and an inspection of the books will show, how every dollar and every cent has been expended, by whom, and for what purpose. No department of the civil government has a system of more exact accountability ; no mercantile house has more certainty and clearness in its receipts and payments. It is true, that to effect these results, care and labour are required ; but the example set by Ezra and his companions teaches us, that the most exact account should be kept of the funds of the Church. Ezra, viii. 24–34."

EXTRACTS FROM ANNUAL REPORTS.

The Annual Reports of a Missionary Board are important documents. They may be regarded as missionary "state papers." They may well be referred to in these memoirs, especially when they relate to the early years of the Society or Board.

The first four of these Reports were written, all but the last, and it chiefly, by the Rev. Dr. Elisha P. Swift, Secretary of the Western Foreign Missionary Society, and bear ample witness to his ability and admirable Christian character. These Reports are for the years 1833–36. The Report of 1836 from May 1st, and the Report of 1837, of the W. F. M. Society, the fifth of its series, were written by Mr. Lowrie, as well as the subsequent Annual Reports for many years of the Board of Foreign Missions of the General Assembly. For particulars of the first five reports see Dr. Ashbel Green's Presbyterian Missions.

In the First Report of the Board to the General Assembly, 1838, Mr. Lowrie wrote : "It is for the judicatories of the Church to take the oversight of this great interest. The brethren among the heathen can be formed into Presbyteries under the direction of the proper Synods; and when the number of Presbyteries make it expedient, the General Assembly can form them into one or more Synods in connection with itself.

"Other branches of missionary labour will consist in translating and printing the Bible, and religious tracts and publications; and when practicable taking the oversight of common education, and in all cases giving it encouragement. These duties may vary in their relative importance according to the circumstances of the different missions, and the calls and openings of Divine Providence; and the extent to which they may do so must be left to the judgment and discretion of the missionaries, under the general direction and advice of the Board."—*Report of* 1836.

RESPONSIBILITY OF THE BOARD.

"If there were but a single church, or a few churches near each other, engaged in sending one or more missionaries, nothing more would be needed than their thus engaging in the work. But if the churches willing to be thus engaged are numerous, then an intermediate agency is found most convenient to transact the business between these united churches and the missionaries, and to be the principal medium of communication between both. This medium of communication is found in the Missionary Society [or the Board]. But it is of vital importance to bear in mind, that the members of the Missionary Board are not the principals in this matter; they are themselves but the agents of the churches, appointed by them, responsible to them; and should they neglect their duty, may be, and ought to be, displaced and others appointed in their stead. The missionaries sent out are not their missionaries, but belong to the churches sending them and supporting them with their funds, and sustaining their hands by their prayers. This control over the Missionary Society, or Board, by the churches, can be efficiently exercised, where the organization of the Society is ecclesiastical. If an evil exists in the management of the institution, the remedy is easy. The Church, through the General Assembly, can remove the whole Board, and commit the trust to the hands of others."—*Annual Report,* 1837.

MISSIONARIES—MESSENGERS.

"Every foreign missionary is a messenger sent by a church, or by churches, to carry to the heathen, or un-evangelized, the gospel of the risen Saviour. This simple proposition involves some very important and peculiar relations between the missionary abroad and the Church at home; and on these relations some of the most important and vital principles, in conducting the missionary operations, will be found to depend.

"On the part of the missionary, this relation requires that he give himself entirely to the work; that he receive instructions from the Church, in reference to his field of labour, and his duties in that field; that he is to keep the Church advised of his progress, of his encouragements, and of his discouragements; that he is to use with all economy and discretion the funds put into his hands; and further that he is to preach the same gospel to the heathen which the

Church at home receives. On the part of the Church, this relation requires that they furnish their messenger with a comfortable support; that they see to it that he be sound in the faith, lest instead of truth he disseminate error among the heathen. Above all it is the duty of the Church, 'with one accord,' to bear their messenger daily before a throne of grace, that having performed the part of the human agency, they may look for the blessing of the Holy Ghost sent down from heaven, to rest upon the labours of their missionary."—*Annual Report*, 1836.

PREACHING THE GOSPEL BY NATIVE CONVERTS.

"The first instruction to be given to all missionaries is to preach the gospel of Jesus Christ. To the Jew this may be a stumbling-block, and to the Greek foolishness, but to them which are called, both Jews and Greeks, Christ the power of God and the wisdom of God. Let no Missionary Society place any other agency above that of the living preacher, lest they be found wise above what is written.

"Next to the direct preaching of the gospel, the attention of the missionaries must be strongly called to the importance of rightly using all proper human means for raising up a qualified native ministry. On this part of the subject it is believed that a serious mistake has existed, even in the minds of most devoted friends of foreign missions. The agency of a native ministry has been overlooked, and the most pressing calls have been made on the churches to supply pastors, and provide for their support, for the whole heathen world. But in the experience of every Missionary Society, no truth is more clearly indicated than that the conversion of the heathen must be effected principally by ministers from the heathen themselves. An experienced missionary writing from Africa says, 'You may as well attempt to supply the people with bread from England and the United States, as to supply them with all the ministers they want.' Another writing from India says, 'Did a native missionary possess the same knowledge and the same grace as a European, he would be worth ten Europeans. In knowledge of the language, in access to the natives, in capacity for enduring the heat of the climate, in the expense of his education and support, and in the probability of the continuance of his life, there is no comparison.' This view of the subject is abundantly sustained by many others most experienced in the work of preaching the gospel in person to the heathen. Such also we find was the practice of the first missionaries, when they went out from Jerusalem to make known the Gospel to all the world. In following their example in this and in all other matters, no Missionary Society need fear any mistake."—*Annual Report,* 1837.

MISSIONARIES IN CHINA.

The first missionaries to the Chinese, Rev. Messrs. Mitchell and Orr, and Mrs. Orr, were not permitted to continue in their chosen work, by reason of death in one case and illness in the other. They surely gained a blessed reward of their sacred purpose. The faith of the Missionary Board's Executive Committee and its secretary did not fail, nor the interest of the churches in the projected mission. Moreover, quite a number of excellent young ministers were led by

the Holy Spirit to offer their services for this still un-
occupied field of labour. Prior to, and in, 1844, the
Rev. Messrs. Walter M. Lowrie, M. Simpson Culbertson, Thomas L. McBryde, John Lloyd, Hugh A. Brown,
Andrew P. Happer, Augustus W. Loomis, Richard
Q. Way, and two medical missionaries, James C.
Hepburn, M.D. and D. Bethune McCartee, M.D.; five
of them were married. Ordained missionaries were
also sent to China in later years, until this country is
now the largest mission-field of our Church, as it is
also in population. Among the missionaries have
been some of the ablest men in the Presbyterian
ministry, as also is the case in other missions. All
the ordained missionaries of the Board are appointed
after the special recommendation of their respective
Presbyteries. One of the men who may be specially
mentioned was the Rev. M. Simpson Culbertson,
D.D. His acknowledged standing at the U. S. Military Academy would have led to his eventually taking rank as one of the chief generals of our armies,
some years later, if he had remained at home ; but in
answer, as we may believe, to his widowed mother's
prayers, he was led to go from the U. S. Army in
1841 to Princeton, and thence in 1844 to Ningpo and
Shanghai. His death, after eighteen years of missionary life, in the forty-fourth year of his age, was a
great loss to the mission ; but he never regretted his
consecration to this service.

Of the early missionaries to China, the Rev.
Walter M. Lowrie, the third son of the secretary,
may also here receive special mention. He went to
China in 1842, in the twenty-third year of his age,
after having received the usual collegiate and theological seminary education and ordination by the

Second Presbytery of New York. Of first honours, and valedictorian at college, he was yet so unassuming, so attached to his family and to his friends, and so full of life and energy, as to be a great favourite among them all. By direction of the Board, on his arrival at Macao, he embarked for Singapore, to aid in transferring the work there to China. On this voyage the ship was wrecked on a submerged rock, and, though a fine vessel with an able captain, he and the crew, with a few passengers, barely made their escape in two small boats. They found themselves four hundred miles from land, and poorly supplied with water and provisions. Almost incredible danger and suffering were encountered before they reached Manila—all saved but four men out of twenty-nine. The narrative of this shipwreck in his memoir is one of intense interest. Few that meet such dangers live to report them.

On arriving again at Macao, Mr. W. M. Lowrie continued his study of the Chinese language; aided the printer in his work for the printing-press and its metallic type; visited Hong Kong, Amoy, Chusan, Shanghai, and Ningpo, and settled in the last city as his station, after correspondence with the Board and conference with the missionaries. He could now preach with little aid from an interpreter. His proficiency in the study of the language led his brethren to appoint him as their delegate to a conference at Shanghai of the leading missionaries in China, for the revision of a translation of the Scriptures into Chinese; and he was able to take a modest, but appreciated, part in this work.

After spending a couple of months at the convention, he was requested by his collegues at Ningpo to return to that station on a short visit for some special service.

DEATH OF REV. W. M. LOWRIE.

On this journey he met with his death, under the most distressing circumstances. Accompanied by his faithful Ningpo servant, and another Ningpo man in the employment of the Ningpo Mission, they took the inland journey, which required the crossing of Chapoo Bay in a small native craft. A Chinese piratical barque soon bore down on this small boat for purposes of plunder. At first they did not molest the foreigner, whom they found on board ; but, probably fearing that his presence might endanger their own safety, after a little consultation among themselves, they threw him overboard, and kept him from returning by their spears. His bible, which he was reading while they were plundering the boat, he threw on deck as he was forced over, and it was secured by his servant. It is still in service by a member of his family. Other incidents were reported by his Chinese servant. Evidently his mind was kept in peace until the end came. That end was surely a blessed one, after sorrowful and great tribulation.

NOTICES OF HIS MEMOIRS.

It was on Monday morning, December 17, 1847, that the sad news reached the Mission House, New York, just as the members of the Executive Committee were assembling for their regular weekly meeting. After the meeting was constituted, the Committee agreed to transact no business, excepting to have the letters from China read, and then to spend some time in prayer. The members then adjourned in deep sorrow and sympathy.

A memoir was prepared by his father, which passed through several editions. Some sixty pages of the volume were omitted in the later editions, perhaps to lessen the cost, consisting of "Letters from Missionaries and Others." Their omission is a cause of regret. Seldom is a collection of letters of sympathy and mourning, so sorrowful and yet comforting, from so many missionaries, and from friends in England and our own country, found in a single volume. Particular reference may be made to the "Remarks" on this sad event by the venerable Archibald Alexander, D.D., to the letter of the Rt. Rev. W. J. Boone, D.D., of the American Episcopal Mission, of Shanghai, to many letters from other friends, and to the able review of Mr. W. M. Lowrie's life by the Rev. Richard W. Dickinson, D.D., in the *Missionary Memorial*, of 1852.

It may be added here, that Walter's younger brother, Reuben, after completing his college and seminary course of study for the ministry, went as a missionary to China, and was stationed at Shanghai. He went out to assist his brother as he had expected, but now to take his place; but he was early called to rejoin him in the Saviour's presence. He was permitted to live at Shanghai from 1854 to 1860, and then departed this life, greatly lamented by the missionaries of all the churches in Shanghai. He had declined medical advice as to returning to this country on a visit for his health, saying that he would not return "until he had looked Death in the face." Alas, it was then too late. His wife returned to this country for the education of their children, and then went back to China, at her own charges. She was accompanied by her surviving son, the Rev. J. Walter Lowrie, and her daughter, afterwards married to a medical missionary from New York, also in work at his own charge.

SIAM AND LAOS.

The missions to the Siamese and the Laos received earnest consideration from the Board, at the time when its work for China was undertaken, at Singapore. Mr. Orr made a visit from Singapore to Bangkok, to make inquiries on this subject, influenced partly by the number of Chinese then living in Siam. Mr. and Mrs. Buell afterwards were sent to Bangkok, but the ill-health of Mrs. Buell compelled their return to their home in this country. Others were sent to the Siamese, whose king was unwilling to have them stay. His death, and the accession to the throne of a liberal and friendly ruler changed greatly the prospects of the Mission. Two of their members, Rev. Messrs. McGilvary and J. Wilson, some time later, went to the Laos country. Of late years their ranks have been largely increased. The number of the missionaries should be still further enlarged. Their work has been attended with remarkable encouragement. Notices of the Laos mission, however, belong chiefly to a later period. In the Siamese field proper, valuable labourers—Dr. and Mrs. Mattoon, Dr. and Mrs. McDonald, Dr. House and Mrs. House, and others, have occupied this field ; but not with equal encouragement as among the Laos. For particulars, reference may be made to the paper on Siam, by the Rev. J. F. Dripps, D.D., in the *His-*

torical Sketches, pp. 207–232. Its account of Buddhism—the religion of many in Siam—is one of the ablest on the subject. Dr. N. A. McDonald's " Siam, its Government, Manners, and Customs," is one of the best brief books of reference. It is noteworthy that in both these countries the missionaries are all members of the Presbyterian Church.

EVANGELISTIC WORK FOR THE JEWS.

An interesting part of Mr. Lowrie's official duties related to a mission to the Jews. It had been referred to early and repeatedly in the proceedings of our ecclesiastical courts, as a work requiring almost special attention by the Church. To preach the gospel to the ancient people of God was the first work of our Saviour and His disciples ; but even in those days the followers of our Lord were early taught to preach the gospel to every creature—to the Jews certainly and also to the Gentiles—the world over. The Board and its executive officers so understood this duty. There were then some thousands of Jews in this country, widely scattered in many cities, increasing in number, but difficult of access. Missionaries to them needed special linguistic gifts, and special measures of faith and patience. Some station in Europe or Western Asia was supposed to give access to the greatest number of this unsettled people. To find the right man for this work, and to obtain the funds required for his support, were causes of delay ; but special pecuniary gifts were offered, and a young graduate of the Alleghany Theological Seminary, a native of Ohio, was obtained for this service in 1846, —the Rev. Matthew R. Miller.

Before leaving this country, it was concluded that a year spent in New York, living in some German family, and, if practicable, a Jewish family, and perfecting his acquaintance with Rabbinical Hebrew and his knowledge of the Talmud, under the instruction of a Jewish rabbi, would be expedient. This led to a more thorough knowledge of the home field for this mission, and the decision to make New York its headquarters. Two years later, the Rev. John Neander, formerly a Jewish rabbi in Germany, was appointed a missionary of the Board, the funds for his support having been offered by a generous donor. Mr. Neander's testimonials were considered ample by the Presbytery, and as an acceptable preacher in German, the Board consented to his collecting a small German congregation, not omitting his visits to Jews, and thereby increasing his usefulness. This led to his work becoming to some extent parochial in the home field, successful, but hardly in the Board's sphere. To the end of his life he was revered as a devoted and useful minister of the gospel. Mr. Miller resigned his appointment in 1852, on account of impaired health, to the Board's sincere regret. He was a minister of marked ability and devotedness. Three more brethren of Jewish race were appointed on recommendation of Presbyteries—one in Baltimore, one in Philadelphia, and one in New York. They did not continue many years in this service. The work for the Jews has not been continued by the Board since 1876. Perhaps it should be. Not a few of the ministers and members of our Church feel a special interest in their evangelization; and, as a people, the Jews are still a race of foreigners.

In 1845, the Board entered on missionary work in
Europe. Its importance and its proposed methods
were stated by Mr. Lowrie in the annual report for
that year. Previously there had been considerable
discussion in the Church on the general subject of
missions to the Roman Catholics, whether at home or
abroad. The proposal to organize a separate Board
for this work had been extensively advocated; and
to a less extent, the plan of a Bureau with its separate
secretary, in connection with the Board of Foreign
Missions was also advocated, but not endorsed
by the General Assembly. Neither was the proposal
of a separate Board endorsed, while yet it was felt by
many influential members of the Church, that action
of some kind was called for. The Foreign Board
shared this feeling in general; and with reference to
further measures for making the Gospel known to
Roman Catholics, whether at home or abroad, was
led to appoint one of its ablest and best known
ministers as a resident missionary in France. This
appointment was held in reserve by him until his
return from a visit to Europe which he was soon to
make; and then it was declined by him. Soon afterwards
several lay members of the Executive Committee
spent some time without concert on visits to
Europe, particularly on the Continent, and they were
led to study this subject with care.

When this question came before the Executive
Committee again, all the members were in favor of
missionary work on the Continent, but on certain
lines, to wit: not of sending missionaries from this
country, but of sending pecuniary aid to native

brethren connected with local missionary organiza-
tions in Paris and Geneva, and afterwards also in
Brussels and by the Waldensian Synod for Italy.

The General Assembly cordially approved of this
method of evangelistic work for Roman Catholics as
well adapted to the state of the case in Europe, and
also as indirectly favourable to such work on our continent. On this basis, our connection with our European brethren was maintained from 1845 until 1891.
It was then suspended, under some misapprehensions,
it must have been, as to another method in its stead.
In the preceding nearly fifty years, the Board had
sent over $200,000 to the aid of "Missions in Papal
Europe." The journals and letters received, though
sometimes discouraging, were often of great interest.

The Protestant Churches in the United States cannot look on the efforts of the Romanist Church to
secure again its ascendency in such countries as
France, Belgium, Italy, etc., without deep sympathy
with our few Protestant brethren in those countries.
Already this conflict extends to our own country.
The Papal control of the destinies of the United
States is earnestly sought for. Of $706,455 con-
tributed *for all* Romanist missions, more than half
of this sum contributed by France, $207,215 was sent
to the United States, a larger outlay than for any
other quarter of the globe. . . . But this hostile
action is specially directed against Protestant missionary enterprises. . . . Referring to this conflict, the Board's report of 1845 says :

"On the other hand, a standard has been lifted up
against the enemy. Two efficient societies have been
organized, one in Paris, the other in Geneva. (A
Christian missionary church was afterwards organ-

ized in Brussels, and the venerable Waldensian
Synod was enabled to enter on vigorous evangelistic
work for Italy.)   To take the direction of these
societies, God has raised up able and faithful men,
known to the churches in Europe and in our country,
and possessing in a high degree the confidence of all.
The presence of the Spirit of God is further evidenced
by His blessed influence on many hearts.   The present state of the Church in France is most remarkable.
At this time the Romish clergy are losing power, the
people are leaving them, not by individuals merely,
but by hundreds ; entire villages have ceased from
attending mass, and call for the preaching of the
Word." . . .   The report adds : "In view of this
deeply interesting field of labour, the Committee is
thankful to report that during the last summer a
correspondence has been opened with the Evangelical
Society of Geneva, in the first instance through the
Rev. Dr. Merle d'Aubigne, and with the Evangelical
Society of France, through Rev. Messrs. F. Monod
and J. J. Audebaz, respected pastors of churches in
Paris.   The plan by which the Presbyterian Church
can render effective aid in France and other Papal
countries is very simple.   The excellent directors of
these societies will take charge of any funds remitted
to their care, and apply them agreeably to the wishes
of the donors.   Thus the missionary labourers will be
chosen and directed by those whose local position
and experience enable them best to perform that
responsible duty, and whose well-known Christian
character affords the best guarantee for its faithful
fulfillment.   By this arrangement, the embarrassment,
the greater expense and the less efficiency of labourers from a foreign country will all be avoided.   The

sum of $100 to $120 will support a female or male teacher ; $200, a colporteur for a year, or $80 for five months ; $250, an evangelist ; and $350 or $400, a minister. Funds can also be transmitted for the purchase of libraries of religious books for village congregations, and for the support of young men who are preparing for the work of the holy ministry."

MISSIONS AMONG INDIAN TRIBES.

THE missions of the Presbyterian Church to the American Indians date in 1741, and among the earliest missionaries were David Brainerd and his brother John Brainerd. Other missionaries entered on the same good work; see Dr. Ashbel Green's "Presbyterian Missions." Of the Indian Missions conducted since 1832 by the W. F. M. Society, and by the Board of F. M., the Chickasaw, Seminole, Creek, Choctaw, Wea, Iowa, Sac, Fox, Kickapoo, Otoe, Omaha, Winnebago, Dakota, Chippewa, Ottowa, Seneca, Tuscarora, Alleghany, Nez Perce, Navajo and Pueblo tribes. In some of these tribes, the Seneca, Tuscarora, Alleghany, Dakota, Nez Perce, Choctaw, missions had been previously conducted by the American Board, but most of them had become Presbyterian. Some tribes had been taught by Synods prior to 1832.

It is stated by Professor Garritt, that in forty-eight years our Foreign Board supported 453 missionaries of all classes among the above-mentioned tribes, at an expense of $525,600 by our churches, and of $520,000 entrusted to the Board by the Government for educational work. Over 3,000 persons were received during that time as communicants, exclusive of nearly 2,000 more transferred by the American Board with its Seneca, Dakota, Cherokee and other missions. At least 6,000 children were taught in the schools by the missionaries. Over thirty ministers, licentiates and other native labourers were in the service of the

Board. The clerical missionaries usually acquired a knowledge of the language of the tribes respectively. This knowledge being as needful to them as the languages of Africa or Siam to missionaries in those countries. Not a few of the lady teachers also became proficient in this knowledge. A historical sketch of these Indian missions, by the Rev. Prof. J. B. Garritt, published by the W. F. M. Society, 1334 Chestnut street, Philadelphia, is valuable for reference.

It is not needful to state how these divinely blessed missions ceased to be connected with the Foreign Board. Mr. Lowrie felt a deep sympathy for the Indian tribes, partly from his knowledge of them acquired in the Capitol; and his acquaintance with farming, school-teaching, etc., qualified him for special usefulness in his visits to the Indian settlements. As secretary he made visits, in different years, to eleven tribes—of which two were east of the Mississippi River, and the others lived in territories southwest and northwest of the Mississippi and Missouri. These journeys, west of these rivers, were mostly made on horseback, extending many hundreds of miles, and sometimes subjecting him to severe fatigue, exposure, and even peril—in several cases when he was from sixty to over seventy years of age. But he felt it to be a real privilege to meet the missionaries in their homes, and to address the Indians through an interpreter in their councils or at the stations. It need hardly be added that these visits were warmly welcomed by the missionaries, and by some of the Indians, by their few churches, and by some of the chiefs.

From his journal of a visit in 1852 to the Choctaw,

Chickasaw, Seminole and Creek Missions, in the Indian Territory, requiring absence from the Mission House from April 12th to June 26th, and travelling in the Indian country, mostly on horseback, some 600 miles, a few extracts are here inserted; see *H. and F. Record*, of September, 1852, pages 272–280.

Several days were spent at Spencer, the Choctaw station; for the Chickasaws, Wapanucka was the next station; then Oak Ridge, Seminole; and then Tallahassee and Kowetah, Creek. At all, the usual conferences and religious services occupied the time. The heavy storms of rain and swollen rivers and creeks made the travelling very severe.

Friday, May 21, 1852.—Although the sky was overcast, being anxious to be on my way, concluded to set out. Mr. Allen went with me, intending to return when he saw me across the Canadian branch of the Arkansas, 35 miles distant. We left at 7½ A. M., the horses in fine spirits, and the ride over the prairies for some hours was delightful. At 10 A. M. we reached the Boggy river, but the stream was so deep and rapid, and the banks on both sides so steep, it was impossible to cross, even by swimming the horses. We then concluded to ride some distance up the river, in hopes of getting a better fording. But the river was so crooked that when we were four or five miles up, it was a great distance from the prairie on which we rode. It was now 11 A. M., and a heavy thunder-gust, with rain and wind came upon us. We had just time to put on our Indian blankets, when the rain fell in torrents. I never saw till now such large drops of rain, and so close together. As we rode on we came to a large branch of the Boggy, which took our horses to the belly. We had some misgivings about being able to re-cross this stream, in case we had to return, but hoping soon to reach the main river, we went on. We found, as we advanced, that we had got but the wing of the storm. The little streams were full of water, and every path in the prairie overflowed. The ground was so wet, the horses sunk often to the pastern joint. The Indians whose cabins we passed could not speak English, so we could not learn how far we were from the river. At noon we came to a small stream, not more than twenty feet wide, but so full of water, and so rapid, we could not cross over it. We then turned back, and after letting our horses graze for half an hour, we passed on homewards, as fast as the wet ground, and our now tired horses would permit. Before we reached the first branch, we came to the cabin of Mr. Wilson, a friendly Indian, known to Mr. Allen, and who spoke English. He told us he had just come up from the branch, that we could not cross it, for it was full from bank to bank. He would go with us, however, and he thought, by going round, we could cross it where it forked into three branches. He led us a wide and weary circuit; stayed with us till we crossed two of the forks, and then pointed out the course that would bring us to a path, adding—you cannot lose the road. We did lose it, however, or rather we never found it, and we soon came to the bottom land of the third fork, where we were entangled with grape-vines, green briars, and sharp spines of the Red River burdock. We made various attempts to cross, but in every instance found the water so deep the horses would have to swim. Another gust was coming up, and cross we must, or remain in that wet and gloomy bottom all night. Mr. Allen's horse being larger than mine, got over partly by walking and partly by swimming. He carried my saddle-bags, which, being well made, were but slightly wet. My horse, however, had to swim for it, which he did nobly. We crossed in safety, but were wet nearly to the middle, and our boots were full of water. Making out of the bottom to the prairie, and having each a pocket compass, we pursued a course that Mr. Allen knew would strike a path that would lead us home. We had still eight or nine miles to go, and it was now near 4 P. M. We had to cross a high hill, so steep in descent that we had to walk down. At the foot, Mr. Allen picked up a singular petrefaction, and I was putting it in his saddle-bags, which were on my horse, when I found them half full of water. In one end, Mrs. Allen, with considerate forethought, had placed a little bag of ground coffee, and a paper of sugar. The sugar was all melted, and so much of the coffee that it was about the right strength. Though in no laughing humor, the idea of carrying the saddle-bags half full of liquid coffee, five times sweetened, was so ludicrous that we laughed heartily. After a cold and weary ride we reached the mission at 7 P. M. They were all glad to see us back, as they had seen the storm passing in the north. A change of clothes, a cup of tea, and a cheerful fire made us feel at home.

The day's ride, however, was a hard one, both for man and horse. We were eleven hours on the saddle, exclusive of the half hour we let our horses graze. We must have travelled above forty miles, and the deep roads, the frequent crossings of deep and unbridged streams, made it fully equal to sixty miles. But we were truly thankful that the providence of

God watched over us. Had we not met with Wilson, we must have remained in the forks of the Boggy all night, with no shelter but two wet blankets, and our common clothes. Nothing remains but for me to stand still till these waters subside. I cannot return even, for the waters on the road are up also. In the meantime, were it not for the delay, the home with these dear friends is a very pleasant one.

Saturday, May 22.—Sore enough this morning, and no wonder, for Mr. Allan complains of being sore all over. It rained heavily in the night, and every time I awoke, I thought of the forks of the Boggy, where, but for the providence of God, we would have been passing the night.

May 23 *to* 25.—Had an attack of fever which gave way to medicine. The waters so much fallen. Made arrangements to try the road again to-morrow.

Wednesday, May 26.—Rained very hard all night. Wapanucka creek is over all its banks. The streams are now higher than ever. No way of getting either back or forward. Feel sometimes almost discouraged. No chance of getting twelve miles either way till the waters fall.

Monday, May 31.—Set out again for the Seminole mission, with Mr. Allan and an Indian guide. We reached the Boggy at a point higher up than in the former trial. The river was not deep here, and we thought this could not be the much dreaded stream, till we looked up and saw the high-water mark on the trees some twenty feet above our heads. At sundown we reached the Canadian, forty-four miles from Wapanucka. Our horses suffered much from the prairie fly. My horse being an iron grey, suffered the most, as that is one of their favourite colours.

From 9 A.M. till 4 P.M., he was kept in a constant fever of excitement.

The prairie fly is a beautiful insect; it is about half an inch long, and three-sixteenths of an inch in thickness. Its colour is bright green, and the wings are two-thirds the length of the body. It strikes its victim with the directness of an arrow, and instantly inflicts a deep wound, from which the blood will ooze out in drops, even after the fly is removed. Had I been two weeks later in the season I could have travelled only at night, as thousands upon thousands of them were seen on the weeds and grass in the prairies, not fully fledged.

We lodged at the cabin of a Shawnee Indian with a large family of children. We found on inquiring that there were forty families of Shawnees settled together. Our host could speak pretty good English and was willing to talk. His knowledge of God and divine things was very obscure. When asked if his neighbours would attend to hear preaching and prayer, if a missionary came to them, he did not seem to know what the question meant. Would the parents send their children to school? He could not say; it had never been spoken of. Would they be afraid if a white teacher came to them? No, they were not afraid of white men, why should they? How many children were there belonging to the forty families? He did not know; some had four, some six, some eight or ten; some were young men and women, some little children.

He treated us very kindly; he has been here ten years, and has a large improvement, many horses, and cattle and even goats. His cabins, however, were so small that he made our beds out of doors, with buffalo skins and Indian blankets. But the mosquitoes were so numerous that I slept none the whole night.

1. Little need be added to show the vital importance of the measures here proposed, for the benefit of the Chickasaw people. But unless the qualified men and women can be obtained, these institutions cannot be commenced. A deep responsibility rests upon our brethren in the ministry in regard to this matter. With their assistance the proper agents can be obtained, and no time is to be lost, for some of them are wanted now, and all will soon be needed on their field of labour.

2. It is cause of encouragement that the whole time of one faithful missionary is given to the preaching of the Gospel among this people. Another is greatly needed in the same kind of itinerant labours. Besides the Chickasaws and the Choctaws, there are the forty families of the Shawnees, who have never heard of salvation. Who will go to preach unto them the unsearchable riches of Christ?

3. The blessings of a strong mission among the Chickasaws will not be confined to them, but will in due time extend beyond their limits, and reach the tribes to the south, and far to the west. God in His providence has given this people the means of improvement, and the disposition to use them, by inviting to their assistance those who are abundantly able to instruct them. These institutions, accompanied by the preaching of the Gospel with the blessing of God, will be the means of raising up an educated and sanctified native agency, far beyond their own wants. From this advanced position, the missionaries sent out can be supplied with every facility

for further advances, and accompanied by the native brethren, will in time be able, step by step, to reach the Comanches of Texas, the Pueblas, Apaches and Navajoes of New Mexico, the ancient Cibolos, and even the poor root-diggers of Utah. It was the constant and untiring effort of the Apostle to the Gentiles to preach the Gospel in the regions beyond. This was the rule of his life, so far as he was enlarged and sustained by the churches. So it ought to be with the ministers and the churches now.

SEMINOLE MISSION.

June 1.—Early on Tuesday we crossed the Canadian without difficulty, though the water came above the skirts of the saddle. From bank to bank the river here is half a mile wide, and about half that distance was now covered with water. Here Mr. Allan and the Indian guide returned, and I pursued my way alone, at first through the wide forests which adjoin the river, and afterwards through prairies interspersed with woodland. I could get no guide, however, and soon lost my way among the numerous Indian paths. I had not been able to ascertain whether the Seminole mission was to the northwest or the northeast of the point where I crossed the river. The account I had received of the distance also varied from fourteen to twenty-four miles. After wandering among the paths for more than two hours, I struck a wagon road, and at a venture took the west end. This soon brought me to an Indian settlement, but they could not speak English. When I asked the road to Edwards's store, they always pointed to the road leading to the west. After travelling sixteen miles, I met an intelligent Shawnee Indian who could speak English. He informed me that I was on the California road, going in the wrong direction. I then found I had to go back over these long and weary miles. The heat of the sun was most oppressive, and the flies kept my poor horse in a ferment in every prairie. At sundown I reached Edwards's store, faint and wearied, for I had eaten nothing all day. I had travelled forty-eight miles, and was distant but ten miles from where I had parted with Mr. Allan ; yet I felt truly thankful that, in the providence of God, I had met this friendly Indian. Without his direction I must have gone further out of the way, and have been obliged to lodge in the prairie, without food or company.

Wednesday, June 2.—I reached the Seminole mission at Oak Ridge, at 9 A. M. It is less than fifty miles from Wapanucka, but by the circuit we made to cross the Boggy river, and by losing my way, I had travelled more than one hundred miles.

I found the mission family well, but very uneasy on account of my long delay. After speaking to all the scholars, I spent the rest of the day in viewing the premises and in conferring with the missionaries. The site of Oak Ridge is well-chosen for health, and the woodland and prairies, for miles around, are rich and productive. The buildings, owing to the difficulty in getting boards, are not yet finished, and in their present state subject the families to much inconvenience. When finished they will accommodate thirty scholars. At present, the school contains sixteen Seminoles, supported by the mission, and four Creeks, supported by their parents.

There is but little difference between the Seminole

and Creek languages. Living as these two tribes do, in the same territory, they must at some time become one people. The Seminoles are much scattered, and show as yet but little disposition to attend on religious services; though a few living near attend the public worship on the Sabbath. The boarding-school appears to be the best agency at first, to bring the blessings of the Gospel and civilization to them, and if it were enlarged to thirty Seminole children, it would in due time be to them a rich and precious blessing.

I was so pressed for time, I could stay but little more than one day at the Seminole mission, and on Thursday at 11 A. M., I set out for Tallahassee. Gilbert Combs, one of the largest boys of the school, went with me, to act as interpreter, in case of need. The road lay principally through prairies, and until 4 P.M., the flies stung my horse almost to frenzy. Then two very heavy gusts, or rather torrents, of rain, the second succeeding the first at a short interval, with strong wind, and tremendous thunder and blinding lightning, came down upon us in the prairie. It continued to rain all the evening, and every little rivulet was soon running so full of water we could hardly cross it. Till 9 P. M., we had come to no human habitation, and then we came to a creek so deep and rapid we could not cross. Our condition was now most unpleasant, as it was still raining. The evening was dark, although the moon had been up for half an hour. After such heavy rains, it was impossible for us to kindle a fire, destitute, as we were of an axe, to procure dry wood. Just then we discovered an Indian cabin. A single Indian was in bed, and he permitted us to stay all night. He, too, had got wet, and as a kind Providence ordered it for us, he had left a good fire burning. This was what we most needed, for all my clothes were wet, and those in my saddle-bags were wet also. Mrs. Lilley had kindly furnished us with ground coffee, and plenty of other provisions. For the first time, I tried my hand at making coffee, and, being wet and cold, we found it excellent. After drying my clothes for some time, I lay down on the floor and slept soundly. I felt truly thankful that the Lord had provided for us this humble shelter.

Friday, June 4.—The morning was clear and lovely, the sun came out in all its brightness, and the air was cool and refreshing. We found that the rain of yesterday had quieted our beautiful but tormenting enemies, the flies, and we made good progress on our way. At noon we crossed the north fork of the Arkansas river. The fording is uneven and rocky, and the water deep and rapid, but we crossed in safety. Near sunset we were stopped by Elk creek, which was full from bank to bank. We lodged in an Indian cabin, clean and neat, owned by an Indian woman, who gave us a good supper and breakfast. In the morning her son took us to a fording higher up, where we crossed without swimming the horses. For ten miles, till we reached the wide forest of the Arkansas river, our winged adversaries marked our poor horses with many stains of blood.

CREEK MISSION.

At noon on Saturday, June 5, we reached Tallahassee, being one hundred miles in two days. We were most cordially welcomed by all the missionaries. They too had become quite anxious about me, having heard nothing of me since leaving Fort Smith, on the 29th of April. If I had not reached them that day, they would have sent on Monday to inquire after me.

The boarding-school at Tallahassee contains forty boys and forty girls. I examined it on different days, during my stay. The children appear remarkably well. While in school they are as attentive to their books, as quiet, orderly and obedient as any scholars need be. Mr. and Mrs. Robertson, and Miss Eddy, have charge of the school, and the scholars are highly favoured with having such competent, experienced and efficient teachers. Miss Stedham also is employed as assistant native teacher. Both scholars and teachers are looking forward with confidence to the July examination. From a thorough examination, they have nothing to fear.

Miss Thompson has the general care of household matters, assisted by Mrs. Reid. When out of school the girls come under their care, and I have never seen two ladies better qualified for such an important trust. The boys, when out of school, are under the care of Mr. Junkin. Much of Mr. Robertson's time also is given to them out of school, and as he has considerable skill in working in wood, his example and instructions in this, as well as in matters of more importance, are of much benefit to them.

The connection of Dr. Junkin with the mission was terminated by mutual consent. His purpose is to reside a mile or more from the mission, and give himself wholly to his profession. In case of sickness, the mission will have his services. He has, in a good degree, secured the confidence of this people, and all

his influence among them will tend to promote their
best interests.

I spent the Sabbath at Tallahassee. Mr. Loughridge had an appointment to preach at a place ten
miles distant, from which he returned at 3 P. M. In
the morning the scholars met in the Sabbath-school,
which presented much the appearance of a Sabbath-
school in one of our churches at home. At 11 A. M.
Mr. Loomis preached by an interpreter ; a few of the
neighbours, principally members of the church, were
present. In the afternoon, I made an address to the
scholars, which was translated by the interpreter,
that all might understand it. After this I made an
address to the mission families, at some length, in relation to the missionary work, its trials, and its certain
and glorious results. These exercises were accompanied by singing and prayer, in English and
Muskogee.

June 8.—On Tuesday at 4 A. M., Mr. Loughridge,
Mr. and Mrs. Loomis, and myself set out for Kowetah, fifteen miles distant. By starting so early, we
stole a march on the prairie flies. I stayed but one
day at this station, which gave me barely time to
examine the school and the premises, and arrange
some prospective matters with the brethren.

The school contains forty scholars ; they are about
the same ages, and are pursuing nearly the same
course of studies, as at Tallahassee. I examined the
different classes, and made to them a short address.
These youth and children are exceedingly promising.
Their religious instruction is constantly and promi-
nently attended to. The mission church is made up
chiefly of those who have been, or now are, scholars of
the school, and with the continued blessing of God

on the labours of these his servants, this branch of the mission, if continued as at present, will be of lasting benefit to this people.

When Mr. Loomis's health will permit, he will conduct the services in the mission church on the Sabbath, thus leaving Mr. Templeton to preach on the Sabbath at different places, where preaching is greatly needed. The evening was spent with these beloved missionaries, till a late hour, in religious conversation in reference to the missionary work.

June 9.—At 8 A. M. I bade farewell to these kind friends, and with Mr. Loughridge returned to Tallahassee. For three hours, the flies, in increasing numbers, tormented our horses, and wearied ourselves. I spent the day in the school, and with Mr. Loughridge, examining the premises and all the details of existing arrangements. It is not necessary to speak of his devotion to the best interests of this people, or of his untiring efforts to do them good. He still possesses their confidence, and richly has he merited it at their hands.

The Muskogee chiefs are not prepared to promote education with the liberality that the Cherokees, Choctaws and Creeks promote it—yet they desire their people to be educated. In withdrawing the allowance from Kowetah, I think it not unlikely they counted a good deal on the Board sustaining the school without expense to them.

June 10.—On Thursday at 10 A. M. I parted with the last company of our missionary friends, after we had committed each other to the protecting care and mercy of our heavenly Father. In every instance these partings have been sad and painful to us all. They ought to remind us that this is not our rest, and that we are but strangers and pilgrims here. Mr. Loughridge accompanied me to Fort Gibson, nine miles distant. On the way, we called on General Mackintosh, B. Marshall, Esq., and Mr. Lewis, three of the chiefs whom I met when here five years ago.

IOWAS—SACS—OTTOES—KICKAPOOS.

Mr. Lowrie and Mr. William Rankin, Jr., treasurer of the Board, made a visit to several missions in the Northwest in 1858—the former then in the seventy-fourth year of his age. Their report of this journey begins at New Orleans in May of that year, where they had been members of the General Assembly, as Elders and Commissioners from the Presbyteries of New York and Newark respectively. It is pleasant to see these narratives of their joint work. Mr. Rankin, a man of ample pecuniary means, for thirteen years in practice as a lawyer in a prominent firm in Cincinnati, was led by his religious convictions to accept the office of treasurer of the Board of Foreign Missions in 1850. In this service he continued until advancing years led to his retirement in 1888—honoured and beloved.

Of the visit to these Northwestern Indians, Messrs. Lowrie and Rankin, after a short stay in St. Louis, on matters of Indian missionary business, arrived at the Iowa and Sac Mission. . . . They were on the same boat from Jefferson City to Doniphan with a detachment of Government troops and their supplies, for their expedition to Utah, to which Mr. Lowrie refers: "We had a view of what is required, even on a small scale, to carry on war. Hundreds of horses, and mules, and yokes of oxen. Artillery and smaller arms, wagons, tents, and military stores with all kinds of clothing and provisions, were landed here, and at other points on the Missouri river. A large body of troops had left the preceding day, on their long march across the plains. These we afterwards passed in an evening encampment on the prairie. In view of such scenes, though on a small scale compared with other military movements, how thankful should we be as a nation, that wars with us are so infrequent; and how earnestly ought the Christian to labour and pray for the time when men shall beat their swords into ploughshares, and their spears into pruning-hooks, and nations learn war no more.

Tuesday, June 1.—Left the Iowa and Sac mission, with Mr. and Mrs. Irwin, for the Kickapoo mission, where we arrived at two o'clock P.M. The mission families were then in good health, though previously they had suffered with chills and fevers. Spent part of the time with Mr. Thorne, arranging and deciding on the improvements yet needed, and designating the amount of expenses for the different objects.

The school had at times as many as twenty-four boys, but it now contained but half that number, and as yet no girls have attended. Their parents use all manner of excuses for keeping the girls at home. The adverse influences existing at the Iowa and Sac mission, exist here in full force, and will require the same action of the Department to control them.

Our visit to this mission, in many respects, was a very pleasant one. Our friends in charge of the interests of the school and mission, have had but little experience or intercourse with Indians. But they are devoted to this work, and willing to contend with trials and discouragements, if thereby they may do good to those whom they were sent to instruct.

Thursday, June 3.—Left for the Ottoe mission, some seventy miles distant, and Mr. and Mrs. Irwin returned home. Mr. Irwin had furnished us with a light carriage, well curtained, and drawn by two horses. Henry Mancrovier, a half-blood of the Blackfeet tribe, about seventeen years of age, went with us, to assist on the way, and bring back the carriage and horses, when we should reach the river at Nebraska City. Bidding our friends farewell, we made an early start, and, on Friday the 4th, reached the Ottoe mission at 10 A.M. On our way we passed the troops encamped on a beautiful prairie ; the tents stretching in long and regular lines ; and the horses and oxen feeding in the distance. The most perfect order and stillness reigned throughout the whole.

We found our friends here, Rev. Mr. and Mrs. Guthrie, Miss Sarah Conover, and the two native assistants, in good health. There was a good deal of business matters to be attended to. A beginning only has been made in the improvements. We remained at the mission till Tuesday, the 8th. On Saturday we visited the Indian village, a short account of which has been drawn up by Mr. Rankin. There were no children in the school, yet the Indians appear to be friendly, and when spoken to, always promise to send their children to the school. Their agent, Major Denniston, had urged them strongly to make no more delay, and they said as soon as they returned from their summer hunt, they would fill up the school. Their hunt, much to their disadvantage, was a failure. The Cheyennes barred their way on one side, and the hostile Sioux on the other, so that they could not reach the hunting-ground, and thus were forced to return empty-handed. The adverse influences here are much the same as at the Iowa and Kickapoo missions, and the same remedial measures will be required to remove them.

Tuesday, June 8.—Set out early for Nebraska City, seventy-six miles distant. Hitherto we had been greatly favoured, in not being detained in crossing the streams. Shortly before we reached them, they were too high to be forded, and soon after we had passed they were again flooded with the heavy rains. We reached the Great Nemaha, thirty-five miles, at two o'clock P.M. We crossed without difficulty, although the waters were too high for perfect safety. Soon after a heavy rain came on, which continued all night, and which stopped our further journeying for that day. Had we been a day later, we could not have crossed till the stream subsided. Next day brought us to the Little Nemaha. Here the crossing was really dangerous, but we got over in safety, with some wetting to our carpet-bags. For eighteen miles the roads were the worst that any of us had ever seen. The ravines and small streams running from the interior to the river, seemed to be nothing but tracts of quicksand ; in crossing them, the horses would sink up to the shoulder. At one place I thought the poor horses were gone, and that they never could struggle through. To make it worse, a cold rain fell in torrents the most of those weary eighteen miles. Our young driver, Henry, got frightened at their plunges, and I had to take the rains myself. This gave me a full share of the falling rain. But a merciful Providence watched over us, and at three o'clock, P.M., we reached Nebraska City, where our land journey was for the present to terminate. The rain continued nearly the whole night.

Thursday, June 10.—The rain had ceased, and we started Henry with the team back to the Iowa mission. By crossing into the States of Iowa and Missouri the road to the mission was good. He reached home in safety. No white boy of his age could have been more competent or careful. The steamer "Emigrant" had just arrived, and we took passage in her for Bellevue, sixty miles distant by water. The wetting of the preceding day brought on a severe chill, which was followed by a fever. I kept my berth all day, and reaching Bellevue at dark, we met Mr. Hamilton at the landing, and were soon at home with his quiet and amiable family.

. . . In my weak state of health, Mr. Rankin rendered efficient assistance in attending to business ; this, indeed, he had done at the different missions. From his being on the ground, and seeing the work and the wants of the missionary labourers, he carried back clearer views of the work itself, than could be given by any description. I was very anxious to visit the Omaha mission, one hundred miles above Bellevue. But the road on the river bottom was almost impassable. The streams were high, and the bridges all carried away by the flood. The ridge road was still open, but it was fifty miles further, and required camping out for at least two nights each way. I waited some days for a boat, but could hear of none going higher up than Omaha City. With much reluctance, I gave up the visit to this mission, and engaged Mr. Hamilton to pay it a visit, and confer with the brethren there on some points of interest to the mission and the school. This labour of love Mr. Hamilton performed, by the first boat that came up after we left.

This mission, though not exempt from the discouraging influence existing at the other missions, is upon the whole encouraging. Twenty-four boys and eight girls are in the schools, while the chiefs and Indians generally appear to place full confidence in their missionaries and teachers.

In this month, Mr. Lowrie turned over some matters of business to Mr. Rankin, and returned to the Mission House, New York. Mr. Rankin's report here follows :

The Ottoe mission is seventy-five miles west from the Missouri river, a few rods south of the fortieth parallel of latitude, which divides the Territories of Kansas and Nebraska. It stands on a rich prairie, with running water near at hand, and with woodland views in every direction. The Mission House, a large three-story building of concrete, is a conspicuous object at the distance of several miles.

Mr. Lowrie and myself, with our Indian boy Henry, of the Iowa school, arrived at the Mission on Friday, the 4th of June, having travelled seventy miles in a two-horse curtained wagon from the Kickapoo mission. The Rev. H. W. Guthrie and wife are here as superintendents, and Miss Sarah Conover as teacher. There are also as assistants, Kirwan Murray and Rebecca, his wife ; Isaac Coe, and Margaret, a Pawnee, all educated at the Iowa school. I may not omit Harriet, the coloured woman, who served so long and faithfully Mrs. Irwin, in her missionary labours among the Iowas, and spoke so affectionately of her. We found here, also, an excellent farmer, engaged by

Mr. Guthrie, whom we hope to retain. He had planted about twenty-five acres in corn and potatoes.

Thus provided with teachers and assistants, and a commodious building, forty or fifty children may be accommodated at the Institution, but from various causes on the part of the Indians, none were in the school at present.

Our arrival at the mission at this time seemed very opportune. Some finishing work about the building was going on. The garden, farm, and pasture-field required fencing, which was in part under way. The experience of the secretary enabled him to modify some projected improvements, and suggest others, and the three days spent here, exclusive of the Sabbath, were most laborously occupied.

In the hope of inducing the Indians to place their children in the school, we made a visit to them at their village, six miles off—Mr. Lowrie having sent word in advance that he was coming to hold a council with their chiefs. The village presented a beautiful appearance in the distance, and much resembled a military encampment. It is located on the edge of a grove, with a large stream (the Blue) running through it, and has a broad open prairie in front, on which a large number of ponies were feeding. We passed two or three graveyards, and saw in one of these picket enclosures, two mourning women by the remains of children, who had died the day before. The dead are buried in a sitting posture, as these cone-like mounds of earth indicate.

The Ottoe tribe numbers eight hundred, and there may have been one hundred tents or lodges. Besides the ponies, there was a goodly supply of dogs. The Indians are very fond of these barking curs, that came about us, and treat them as they do their children, feeding them from the same dish.

Our arrival at the village awakened little interest among the people. A few came around us, but most of them took no notice of the strangers. Groups of men and boys were playing marbles. Others were stretched full length on the grass. Some were fantastically ornamented. One young Indian was passing by on a pony with his head shaved and body painted all over. Not a man or boy was at work. Their cornfield is a little distance off, but it is tilled by the government farmer, and for all other work, when not on their hunt, the women are hewers of wood and drawers of water and bearers of burdens. A number were shifting tents, and I saw one woman bent under a load of tent-poles, that would have weighed down a strong labouring man. Another had upon her back all the utensils of her lodge and its canvass covering. One squaw standing near, turned up to me her infant's face, as it lay in its blanket-bed on her shoulders, and said with a pleasant smile "pappoose." One cannot but admire these Indian children, with their bright, intelligent faces and athletic forms. I do not wonder that our missionary teachers among other tribes become so much attached to them.

I looked into some of the tents. Nothing was to be seen but a little fire in the centre and a few cooking and eating utensils. Men, women and children, with yelping dogs, were sitting or lying on deer or buffalo skins. All wore blankets save some of the younger children, who were naked.

We were disappointed in finding most of the chiefs away on a friendly visit to the Pawnees and

Kaws, and that no general council could be held. But one of them was at home, "Big Soldier," who came up and saluted us. He is a fine specimen of the red race, with an expression of intelligence and energy. He held together with one hand his blanket thrown loosely over his shoulders, while in speaking he gesticulated with the other. Several times when specially animated, the blanket fell off and disclosed a manly form, entirely naked, save a strap or bandage of dressed skin bound round his loins, and rings and beads pendant from three openings slit in his ears.

Mr. Lowrie shook hands with the chief, and introduced to him Mr. and Mrs. Guthrie and myself. He then, through Henry as interpreter, addressed him as follows: "I have come all the way from New York to see you and the other chiefs. I am sorry so many are absent, but am glad to meet you, and find you well. I wanted to see how the mission house gets on, which your grandfather, the President, has built for you. I am surprised and grieved to find that none of the children are in the school. It grieves me to see them here running about naked, or in blankets, when they might be dressed like Kirwan and Henry. These were sent to school, and, as you see, are just like white men. That mission house was built for you, that your children might be taught to work, to speak English, to read and write. Your grandfather wants you to be equal to your white neighbours, to stand up by their side, and not be imposed on. These bright-looking children that I see about me may all become white men and women. These good friends (pointing to Mr. and Mrs. Guthrie) have come here from a great distance to do them good, and to do you good. They will feed, and clothe, and teach your

children. When sick they will take care of them.
If any of your people are sick, let them know it, and
they will come and give them medicine. I expect
soon to visit your grandfather at Washington, and I
will tell him that I have been here—and what do you
think he will say, when he hears that none of these
boys and girls are yet in the school? I think he will
say that you are doing very wrong, and that you
must have no more annuities until your children are
sent to school, and kept there."

Big Soldier replied, that the chiefs would return
in four or five days, and they would then talk over
what had been said. He believed they would send
the children to school. They had better be there than
playing about here doing nothing. Some of them
had been sent, and had run away, because they did
not like to stay. He thought the chiefs would make
them stay. He was glad they were to have medicine,
for yesterday two of the children died. He then
changed the subject. Said that the Pawnees were
coming to make war on them, and take their horses.
Mr. Lowrie told him, that the Pawnees would not
make war on them. Their father, the agent, would
not permit it, and concluded by again referring to the
duty of the chiefs in regard to their children, and
what would be expected of them. We then shook
hands with Big Soldier and a number of others who
were standing about.

It was a sad sight, next to being in an insane re-
treat, to see such childishness on the part of full-
grown men and women. No wonder that these tribes
melt away under the influence of shrewd and unprincipled white men. The power of Christian missions
can alone rescue them from that oblivion to which

they are hastening ; and this fact is doubly apparent
to one who has seen, as I have, the social tendencies
of the "untutored Indian," surrounded by the destructive tendencies of those who care only for their
lands.

What effect this mission is to have upon this degraded tribe, it is of course impossible to say. The
providence of God has cast these Indians upon the
Board. Discouragements met us at the outset, and a
wavering faith would throw off the burden, and leave
a race of men to perish. It would be the first instance
in our history, of the Church deserting those for whose
welfare she had embarked, because of their indifference to their own future. There is success in hope-
ful effort, in perseverance, and in prayer. We
remember discouragements in the early missions
among the Iowas, the Chippewas, and south-western
tribes, but these vanished before the self-sacrificing
labours of the beloved brethren and sisters who went
among them. Our secretary could point with deep
gratitude to those two youths, Kirwan and Henry,
from the Iowa mission, who were with us on this
visit, and make them, as he did, his strongest argument to the naked chief, in behalf of the Christian
education of his tribe. It was unfortunate that the
chiefs were not all present, that he might have ex-
acted of them, in solemn council, a promise that their
children should at once enter the institution. We
live in hope of seeing them there, and of witnessing
the blessing of God upon these Ottoe Indians.

MISCELLANEOUS.

COLLECTING AGENTS OR FIELD SECRETARIES.

THE methods of obtaining funds for the support of missions required careful consideration by the W. F. M. Society, and also by the B. F. Missions in its earlier years. Both had adopted the plan of employing agents for this purpose. Both Dr. Swift and Mr. Lowrie strongly favoured it. In those days it was evidently expedient, and was in general use by benevolent societies and boards. As an example, the American Colonization Society, in Washington, supported by members of all denominations, adopted this method and other methods of similar nature; and when Mr. Lowrie, as an honorary member of its Board of Managers, prepared at their request a report on its embarrassed financial condition, it met with their unanimous approval.—*Seventeenth Annual Report*, 1834, pages 26-37.

The Presbyterian Board was regarded as highly favoured in obtaining the services of the Rev. John Breckinridge, D.D., as general agent in 1838; but an urgent call to a pastoral charge, and his lamented departure from this life, led to the discontinuance of the agency in 1841. The usual agencies, each extending to a few synods, were appointed down to 1855, when they were discontinued. This was the result of discussions in the Church courts and in the religious newspapers, etc. Some of the ablest and best minis-

ters were employed in this service, but it was difficult
to secure such men and difficult to retain them ; besides, it involved an expense amounting to over
$50,000 for salaries from 1838 to 1855. The secretary
and other members of the Executive Committee all
agreed as to the expediency of discontinuing the Collecting Agents or Field Secretaries. Henceforth the
cause of missions was to rest for its pecuniary support on Divine grace, and on our church principles ;
or the doctrine of Christian stewardship, and on the
Apostolic direction in I. Corinthians, xvi, 1. Its
agents were to be the pastors and elders or other
members of the churches. Even in former times they
were the main supporters of the cause of missions.

A GOOD WORKING PLAN.

It is still of great moment to have in each congregation a good working plan for church collections.
An example may be cited, which has proved for
twenty years to be acceptable, efficient and successful. It is briefly this :—1. A collection every Lord's
day. 2. A certain number of collections on successive
days assigned to each cause by the session of the
church, its members having conferred with members
of the church as to this distribution. 3. These
weekly collections to be asked for in three classes :
First, for communion expenses and relief of the poor.
Second, for Providential objects ; none of these being
ordinarily numerous. Third, for the Boards of the
Church. Collections for these Boards to be taken on
so many *successive* Sabbaths for each, as the church
session may appoint. Notice to be given from the
pulpit *on the Sabbath preceding each series*, with a

sermon or statement of the object. This plan has
given great satisfaction. It has special merits. One
of these is that it secures support for all the regular
church objects. Another is that it leaves to each
donor to decide as to the object and the amount of
his or her gifts to the cause of Christ, so far as these
are to be connected with the church. On lately inquiring of the respected pastor of this church—which
is one of the best, though subject to removal of its
members to the city and to the West—as to the success of this plan after so many years, he replied:
"Twenty years ago this church was pecuniarily twice
as strong as it is now; but its gifts are now twice as
large as they were then." In both dates this church
was favored with having the same minister.

Some difference of opinion exists as to the expediency of official visits to the Missions in foreign
countries, by the Secretaries or other agents of the
Board. These visits are advocated on the ground of
their usefulness to both agents and missionaries, in
securing a good knowledge by both parties—as to
each other and as to the subjects which require their
joint consideration—resulting in the adoption of plans
which require the expenditure of funds in greater or
less degree. This personal acquaintance is a matter
of moment, it ought always to be secured before a
missionary goes to his field of labor. In missions of
long existence and matured experience, however,
most questions are likely to be settled by brethren of
the home office and in the field without special visits,
as on both sides they are governed by similar

religious principles of action, aided by the admirable organization of our church courts—especially by the Presbyteries. The social intercourse of home visits by missionaries to this country are often necessary as well as useful. There are difficulties and practical objections to "deputations," however, which stand in the way.

First of all, are they really needed ? Are not the brethren in the field competent for their work ? Consider who they are. Then, these visits are necessarily made in some degree of haste, perhaps hurry. The secretaries, or the visitors, if they are the right men, have their main and great work already in hand at home. Their visits abroad are of limited time, and so are necessarily lacking in thoroughness, at most a sojourn of a day or two with a missionary's family, or at a mission station, all the time probably that can be allotted to it, can seldom be satisfactory—in several respects. The expense of these journeys is also to be considered ; usually amounting to hundreds, sometimes to many hundreds, of dollars. The longer a Missionary Board continues in its administration, the less should be its executive expenditures, *pro rata*, and not the greater. But without dwelling on the *pros* and *cons* of the case, all will concur in the judgment that much depends on the men on both sides. The danger is that of relying too much on the secretaries, and too little on the missionaries.

As germane to this memoir—this subject was very earnestly brought before the Secretary by the early missionaries in China, who requested him to make them a visit, to aid them in settling the grave questions at the beginning of our missionary work in that vast country. *But these matters were happily*

disposed of without the desired visit. The inference
from all is: Single out the right men on both sides;
then trust them, under Divine guidance—each in his
own sphere; in connection with his Presbytery; as a
part of our Church system under the General
Assembly. By "Deputations," no reference is
intended to informal visits to Indian Tribes.

MISSION HOUSE LIBRARY.

In 1840, the senior secretary gave a good deal of
consideration to the forming of a library, for the use
of the missionary rooms. In 1861, such progress had
been made that a catalogue of nearly one hundred
pages octavo was printed, under the title of "A
Catalogue of the Books and Maps Belonging to the
Board of Foreign Missions of the Presbyterian
Church." In the general index these were classified
under Africa, Bibles, Biography, China, Commerce,
Dictionaries, Grammars, etc., Geography, Idolatry,
India, Indians, Miscellaneous, Missions, Periodicals,
Polynesia and Oceania, Voyages and Travels; the
book number preceding each title, and the names of
donors following each gift, respectively. Most of
them were valuable; many of them, rare; some of
them of special interest. It was a collection of books
that amply repaid its founder for the hours secured
from other and pressing labours. His special interest in China had led him to give to this library from
his own collection, and to procure from other sources,
not a few volumes in the Chinese language. In 1844,
a large number of volumes in the same language were
presented to this library by the late Mr. David W.
C. Olyphant, a distinguished merchant of New York,

in the China trade. He had obtained the services of the Rev. Dr. Bridgeman, eminently qualified for the work, to procure these volumes—nearly 2,000 in number. It was a noble gift. And it was noteworthy that two such men should have had the same object in view previous to their personal acquaintance. See extracts from their letters in the *Foreign Missionary Chronicle*, New York, 1844, pages 254, 255.

The Chinese part of the library is supposed to be unusual in this country. Besides Mr. Olyphant's splendid gift, a number of Chinese books were received from other donors. In addition to the books above referred to, there are now many volumes of letters in manuscript, consisting of the correspondence of the Board with its friends at home and the missionaries abroad. Copies of the official letters, the others original—bound, indexed and classified according to date and to the missions respectively. These are official and not public, and they are invaluable.

The friends of Foreign Missions, of course, will not expect this library to become one of the *great libraries*, but, as a collection of books for particular uses, it will be gradually enlarged. The efficient and gratuitous services of Mr. W. Henry Grant, librarian now in the charge of it, under the direction of the Board, will no doubt tend to increase its usefulness.

This collection consists now, in 1895, of about seven thousand volumes.

"CHILDREN'S FUND" $13,000.

This fund, as reported by the Board of Foreign Missions in 1866, owed its existence chiefly to the Secretary's pleading for it in the last years of his life.

Its object was to aid in the support and education of the children of missionaries. This education can seldom be fully obtained among anti-Christian nations, so that the painful separation of missionary parents and children for some years seems to be unavoidable. It is usually the greatest trial of missionary life—a trial in which all Christian parents can give them warm sympathy. It is a trial somewhat mitigated when the mother can accompany her children for a time.

The responsibility of deciding on the plans that should be adopted for the children rests on their parents, and while they are living cannot be transferred to other parties. The main thing is that of *the home* for them; and usually this should be sought in the circle of family relations and friends, where they may enjoy *family* ties and influences, acquaintances, sympathies, occupations, etc., like other children. These relatives may find the extra expense involved to be inconvenient; and a "Children's Fund" may in such cases be quite useful, under the direction of the Missionary Board. Thus far it is the children's *home* that their parents will chiefly consider. The question of their *school* is also important, but less difficult. The number of excellent colleges, boarding academies and seminaries, often ready to admit a scholar or two at reduced rates; their being within easy reach of the resident homes of the scholars for their vacations; climatic conditions, in some cases; lessen the difficulties.

The "Children's Fund" would probably have been much larger if the active years of the Secretary had been prolonged. A pamphlet, published in 1855, no doubt received his consideration: "Remarks on the

Provision that Should be Made for the Children of Missionaries," New York: A. D. F. Randolph. Recently special buildings have been provided at Wooster, and in connection with the college in that city, under the liberal charge and supervision of a number of ladies. It is believed that great good will result from this arrangement.

RE-ELECTION AS SECRETARY DECLINED.

Mr. Lowrie had generally enjoyed good health, and he was accustomed to undertake a large amount of labour. But when he had become over eighty years of age he was subject to infirmities. It became increasingly difficult for him to make journeys, which his office seemed at times to call for, or to remain at his desk without fatigue, as in former years. His judgment was clear that the time had arrived when he should withdraw from public service. Accordingly on the fourth of May, 1865, he addressed a letter to the Board of Foreign Missions, declining a re-election as a corresponding secretary of the Board.

The following Minute was then adopted by the Board :

"*Whereas*, A communication has been received from the Hon. Walter Lowrie, declining, on account of his advanced age, and very impaired health, a re-election as one of the secretaries of the Board ; and whereas he has served the Board in this relation of Secretary for thirty-two years with distinguished ability, untiring zeal, and most conscientious faithfulness, to the unqualified satisfaction of the Church at large, as well as the successive members of the Board, during his protracted term of service : Therefore

"*Resolved*, 1*st.*—That this Board receives his communication with unfeigned regret, and accepts his declinature solely on the ground stated by himself. Knowing, as this Board does, that the value of his past service cannot be overestimated, and that nothing short of physical disability for the duties of the office has constrained him to withdraw from a work for which he voluntarily abandoned an honourable and lucrative position in the Senate of the United States ; and to which, under an irrepressible conviction of his duty and its importance, and with unwavering faith in its ultimate triumph, he consecrated three of his sons as well as himself.

" *Resolved*, 2*d.*—That the Board renders to the Hon. Walter Lowrie its grateful acknowledgments for all his past services, and especially for his gratuitous counsel and aid, during the last three years, to the Executive Committee of the Board ; and in parting with our venerable and honored Secretary we follow him with our warmest wishes and prayers that God's presence may go before him, God's grace succor and cheer him, and at last minister to him an abundant entrance into the heavenly kingdom.

"*Resolved*, 3*d.*—That Mr. Lowrie be invited at his convenience and pleasure to sit as an honorary member of the Executive Committee of this Board."

In the General Assembly of May in the same year, the following Minute was adopted, at the instance of its Standing Committee on Foreign Missions, Rev. Robert J. Breckinridge, D. D., Chairman.

"We have learned with deep regret that the Hon. Walter Lowrie, for so many years the devoted and efficient senior Secretary of the Board, has, on account of his advanced age and impaired health, declined a re-election : Therefore

"*Resolved, 7th.*—That we take great pleasure in recording our high appreciation of the invaluable services of the retiring Secretary, the Hon. Walter Lowrie, and we tender to him our heartfelt thanks and sympathy, praying that the Gospel he has striven for so many years to make known to the perishing may be his all-sufficient consolation in his declining years ; and that, in God's own good time, he may have an abundant entrance ministered to him into the everlasting kingdom of our Lord and Saviour Jesus Christ."

THE LAST ILLNESS AND DEATH.

In the declining weeks of his life the health of Mr. Lowrie became more and more feeble ; it had been remarkably vigorous in his early and middle-aged years. He continued to enjoy the affectionate ministries of his family and friends, and to manifest his usual interest in the cause of Missions, until within a short time of his departure. He then met with a fall on a stairway of his house, which soon afterwards showed that there was severe concussion of the brain, attended with increasing weakness ; but there was no want of love and sympathy for his family. There was no impatience, and no word ever spoken that his friends would regret to hear. His worldly affairs had been all arranged, including a liberal bequest to the Board of Foreign Missions. A touching incident occurred after he had become so weak that one of his sons usually sat up with him for the night. At about two o'clock, when all was quiet and still, he began to speak—evidently under the impression that he was in a Council of Indian Chiefs and others. He continued to speak, keeping steadily on for ten or twelve minutes; his line of remarks showed his usual good sense, and his deep feeling as to their welfare was evident. He entreated them to give heed to the instructions of the missionaries, their best friends; to secure the education of their children; to make a good use of their Christian privileges; especially to look unto the Lord Jesus Christ as their personal Saviour. His voice was gradually becoming feebler, until his remarks were ended. It was an address never to be forgotten by his only hearer.

Not entering on other particulars of his last illness, it is sufficient to say that his last days were in keeping with his life. He entered into rest, December 14th, 1868, in the eighty-fourth year of his age. "Blessed are the dead, which die in the Lord, from henceforth: Yea, saith the Spirit, that they may rest from their labours; and, their works do follow them."

Memorial action was taken in reference to the departure from this life of Mr. Lowrie, by the Executive Committee of the Board of Foreign Missions; by the Presbytery of New York, with which he was connected as an Elder of the First Presbyterian Church; by the Board of Foreign Missions, at its annual meeting; and by the General Assembly of the Presbyterian Church, at its following sessions in 1869.

The minutes of the Executive Committee are here inserted, as representing the views of the excellent and distinguished men with whom he had been in weekly conference for so many years:

Minute of the Executive Committee, on the death of Mr. Lowrie, adopted at their meeting, December 28th, 1868:

It is with feelings of mournful interest that this Committee records this last Minute in reference to the Hon. Walter Lowrie, who fell asleep in Jesus and entered into his rest on the 14th of December, 1868.

In view of the departure of one who, as the Corresponding Secretary of this Board, has been so intimately identified with all its interests for a period of thirty years, and to whose wise and efficient administration it is indebted so largely for its present measures of prosperity—be it *Resolved*,

1*st.* That whilst we bow submissively to this manifestation of the Divine will, we cannot but mourn the loss of one whom we all loved and revered, and to whom, even amidst the infirmities of age, we always looked for wise counsel and safe guidance.

2*d.* That we record our high estimate of the ability with which he managed the affairs of this Board; of the indefatigable industry with which he prosecuted its interests; of the wisdom with which he guided its policy in times of difficulty; of the humble, earnest and prayerful confidence with which he always carried forward the work; of the persuasive and effective eloquence with which he urged the claims of missions upon the churches; and of the self-denial to which he submitted in sacrificing high secular position, in consecrating his fortune and life, and giving his children to be labourers in the great work of the world's evangelization.

3*d.* That we recognize in his death a renewed call of Divine providence to this Board to be earnest and faithful; and to the churches to stand firmly by the cause of missions, and by increased effort and enlarged contributions, to carry forward the work, until the Gospel is preached for a witness to all nations.

4th. That we express to his bereaved family our tenderest sympathy, and the assurance of our earnest prayers, that whilst God sanctifies this affliction to their good, He may also fill their hearts with all the consolations of His grace, and lead them, by an imitation of an example so fragrant with blessed memories, to the same benevolent consecration and the same undying reward.

It was further directed that a copy of this Minute be sent to the family of Mr. Lowrie, and that it be published in the *Record* and *Foreign Missionary*, and other papers.

𝕴𝖓 𝕸𝖊𝖒𝖔𝖗𝖎𝖆𝖒:

THE ADDRESS

DELIVERED AT THE
FUNERAL OF HON. WALTER LOWRIE,
IN THE
FIRST PRESBYTERIAN CHURCH,
NEW YORK, DECEMBER 16, 1868.
BY THE
REV. WM. M. PAXTON, D.D.,
PASTOR OF SAID CHURCH.

PUBLISHED BY REQUEST OF THE EXECUTIVE COMMITTEE
OF THE BOARD OF FOREIGN MISSIONS.

ADDRESS.

" How beautiful it is for man to die
  Upon the walls of Zion, to be called
  Like a watchworn and weary sentinel
  To put his armor off and rest—in Heaven."

" Blessed are the dead which die in the Lord from henceforth : Yea, saith the Spirit, that they may rest from their labours ; and their works do follow them."

" Thou shalt come to thy grave in a full age, like as a shock of corn cometh in in his season."

Such was the death of our departed father. He had long stood as a sentinel upon the watch-tower ; and ever and anon, through the hours of the dreary night, he had answered the inquiry, "Watchman, what of the night?" and now, watchworn and weary, just as the harbingers of the dawn are changing into the promise of noonday, he puts his armor off, "and lies down to quiet dreams."

His watch has ended, and so the Lord hath given "his beloved sleep." Blessed death ! He "died in the Lord," and now, resting from his long life of labour, "his works,"—his work of self-sacrifice for Christ; his work of diligent toil, as he gathered with Him in the harvest ; his work of unflinching fidelity, as he stood with Him in the battle,—follow after him, not as the ground of merit, but as the witness of his fidelity, and as the measure to indicate the proportion of his reward.

He was favored with a long life of uninterrupted usefulness, and now, in full age, with the ripe fruitage of fourscore years around him, he has come to his grave, like a shock of corn in his season.

Few men are permitted as he was to finish his course and fulfill his mission. Human life is but a record of purposes broken off in the midst, and of the unwrought projects of usefulness suddenly arrested. David had it in his heart to build the temple ; but he was to die before his work was fulfilled. Moses and Aaron were charged with the work of leading the tribes through the perils of the wilderness into the promised land ; but they had to rest from their labours ere the work was accomplished. And so it often is. The young man is stricken in the dew of his youth, with the vision of life just opening before him ; the husbandman is called to leave his plow in the furrow ; the artist to leave his half-formed picture on the canvass ; the merchant to leave his business, when fortune is hovering before his grasp ; and the minister to vacate his pulpit, while yet his heart is yearning to gather sheaves into the garner. But to our departed father it was given to labour to the last shades of evening, and to see the great work to which he had given the vigor of his life, rise from the smallest beginning, through perils and difficulties, into prosperous operation and vigorous establishment ; and then, with the promise of higher success rising before him, just as the door of access to the whole heathen world is open, he is permitted to draw the drapery of his couch around him and say, "Lord, now lettest Thou Thy servant depart in peace, for mine eyes have seen Thy salvation." If, when he commenced this work, so feeble and discouraging in its incipiency, it had been given him to know that he would live to see its present measure of success, he would doubtless have said, "This is all my desire." In a modified sense, he might, like the Master Himself, have said, as he laid down his armor, "I have glorified Thee on the earth ; I have finished the work Thou gavest me to do."

And now having, like David, "served his generation by the will of God "—he has fallen asleep.

We cannot look upon such a long life of Christian action and benevolent labour,—without a blemish to impair his usefulness or mar his memory, terminated only by the decay of nature, and closing in the peace and quietude of happy death,—without the profoundest satisfaction. Next to the Bible, A GOOD MAN is one of God's best gifts to the world. He is the salt that counteracts its corruption ; the leaven that is to interpenetrate the masses with vital and saving influence ; the light to dissipate darkness ; the mirror to reflect the image of God ; a fountain of living waters ; a source of blessed and beneficent influence in the whole sphere of his life and action.

When a good man dies, we feel his loss, the *World* feels it, for one on whose account God loves the world is taken away ; the *Nation* feels it, for one who was its strength and security is removed. When Elisha looked with streaming eyes after the ascending prophet and exclaimed, "My Father, my Father, the chariot of Israel, and the horsemen thereof," he uttered in reference to Elijah what is true in reference to every good man, that he is of more value to the nation than munitions of war ; a better protection than chariots and horsemen. But, above all, the *Church* feels the good man's loss ; a voice that prayed for Zion is hushed, a tongue that testified for Jesus is silenced, a mind that thought for Jesus sleeps, a heart that cherished the solicitudes of the kingdom and travailed in birth for souls is stilled, a star that shone upon our darkness is extinguished, a fountain that refreshed the desert is dried up. But no—death does not extinguish the good man's influence. Thousands that are in their graves to-day are working in the memories of the living and producing great effects. There are men who have long since mouldered to ashes with whose names we may electrify a nation and thrill the world. The dead rule the living. Our deeds live after us, rise again and reproduce themselves by the agency of minds which we have helped to form, minds which will form their like in never-ending succession. Does not Walter Lowrie still live? live in the spirit of missions, live in the scores of missionaries who caught from him the spark of glowing zeal ; a spark which has kindled into a flame and is now burning with a steady and ever-extending brightness over the heathen world, and which will cast its blessed radiance upon generations yet unborn.

He being dead yet speaketh. Let us then listen to the voice which speaks to us from out the events of his well-spent life.

Walter Lowrie was born in Scotland, in the City of Edinburgh, on the 10th of December, 1784. At the age of eight years he came with his parents to America.

The family located first in Huntingdon County, Penn., but shortly after removed to Butler County, where they made their permanent residence.

Walter grew up on his father's farm, performing

such labour as the necessities of the times demanded, and enjoying nothing more in the way of education than the home instruction of winter nights, with the addition perhaps of an occasional quarter's schooling under the direction of the itinerant teachers of those early times. His early instruction in the principles and practice of religion was of the most thorough and accurate character. His parents were both pious, and Presbyterians of that genuine intelligent school who believe in the Westminster Confession and Catechism, as the best exposition of the truths of the Bible; and in the covenant obligation which rests upon parents to train their children in the nurture and admonition of the Lord.

His conversion to God occurred in his eighteenth year, during the prevalence of those early revivals in western Pennsylvania, which were distinguished by what was commonly called "the falling exercise." He always spoke with much interest of his recollections of those times, and described his own incipient experiences of religion as connected with these strange exercises.

One of the first evidences of the existence of genuine piety in his heart, was an earnest desire to become a minister of the Gospel. With this view he commenced a course of study under the direction of the Rev. John McPherrin, the first Presbyterian minister in Butler County. In the pursuit of knowledge he manifested the same diligence and persevering determination which has given success to his whole life. After making some proficiency in Latin, he determined to commence the study of Greek, and, as Greek books were at that time very rare, he performed a journey of thirty miles on foot to procure a

Greek lexicon. By persevering industry he attained
to a knowledge of Latin, Greek and Hebrew which
would put to shame many who have all the advan-
tages of an Academic education. Providential circumstances, however, hindered the fulfillment of his purpose to become a minister of the Gospel; but with the
same determination to devote his life to the glory of
God, he entered upon other pursuits. His secular
life was such as to win the confidence and esteem of
the whole community in which he lived. Accordingly, in 1811, at the age of twenty-seven, he was
elected as the Representative of that district in the
Senate of Pennsylvania. This honourable station he
held for seven years, during which time he rose to
such a position in the confidence of the people of the
whole State, that in 1818 he was elected as the Representative of Pennsylvania in the Senate of the United
States. In this position of honour, second only to that
of President or Vice-President, he continued for six
years.

This was a period of great interest in the history
of our country, owing to the importance of the measures then agitated, and the great men whose influence
guided the councils of the nation, Webster, Clay,
Calhoun, Randolph, Benton, and many others scarcely
less illustrious, were members of the Senate, and
their great powers were put forth in the discussion of
the measure well known as the "Missouri Compromise."

Among these distinguished Senators Walter
Lowrie occupied a position of honourable prominence.
His great integrity won their confidence, whilst his
peculiar sagacity and practical judgment led them to
seek his advice and rely upon his opinions. I am

informed, by one who was present at that time, that he was regarded by the Senators who knew him best as an authority upon all questions of political history and constitutional law.

During the discussion of the Missouri Compromise he made a speech, which is described as one of great power and force of argument, in which he took strong grounds against the extension of slavery, and uttered his strong protest against the establishment of slave labour upon a single foot of free territory.

But his influence in the Senate was not only that of a statesman, but also of a Christian. He had been ordained a ruling elder in the Presbyterian Church in Butler, and when he went to the capitol he carried with him the savour of vital godliness. He, with Harmer Denny, Theodore Frelinghuysen, and other pious Senators and Representatives, founded the Congressional Prayer-meeting, which has ever since mingled the influences of prayer and faith with the councils of the nation. He was also one of the founders of the Congressional Temperance Society, and was for a long time a member of the Executive Committee of the American Colonization Society.

At the expiration of his term of service as Senator, he was elected Secretary of the Senate of the United States, in which office he continued for a period of twelve years. During this term of his public life, the Providence of God was preparing him for another sphere.

As a member of the Committee of the United States Senate on Indian Affairs, he became deeply interested in the condition of the savage tribes, and much concerned for their spiritual welfare. About the same time his eldest son devoted himself to the work of

missions, and embarked with his father's benediction
to the mission field in India. In this way his heart
was enlisted, first, for the Indians upon our own
border, and then, for the heathen in distant climes,
whither his son had gone with the word of life.

Simultaneous with this was an ordering of Divine
providence by which he became deeply interested in
the study of the Chinese language. It seemed singular to see a statesman, amid the cares and labours of
public life, rising two hours earlier in the morning to
study the language of a people so distant from us,
and in so little sympathy with ourselves. But such
was the ordering of that strange providence, which
leads us in a way that we know not. Whilst God,
by this combination of circumstances, was preparing
him for his future work, he was at the same time preparing the place which he was to occupy. A small
missionary society, supported by a few synods in the
West, had been organized in Pittsburgh; but its
patronage was small and its sphere limited. This
society, however, under the efficient direction of Dr.
Swift, its first secretary, awakened such an interest
in missions as led to a general desire that the work
should be undertaken by the General Assembly upon
a larger scale, and in behalf of the whole Church.
When at length it was determined to extend the mission work and prosecute it with more vigor, and the
question arose, "who shall take the superintendence
of this great interest," the same providence, which
had prepared the heart of Walter Lowrie for the
work, directed to his election.

Obedient to this call, he resigned his office in the
Senate in 1836, and entered upon this new and untried
field of consecrated labour. The office which he held

in the Senate was of such a confidential and responsible character, that it was unaffected by the changes
of administration in the Government. He had but
two predecessors in office, and both held the trust
until death. His resignation of a position so honourable, so lucrative, and which he could have held for
life, was the occasion of much surprise ; and when he
was asked why he did it, he replied, ''that he chose
the place in which there would be the most sacrifice
and the best prospect of usefulness for Christ.'' The
spirit with which he thus entered upon his undertaking was in itself the augury of success. The work
was new, and encompassed on every side with difficulties. The Church was to be aroused, the spirit of
missions enkindled, the system of operation was to
be organized, fields of labour to be sought, missionaries
to be prepared, and the whole plan and policy of a
vast system, encompassing the ends of the earth, to
be arranged and perfected. But to this work he
brought a heart prepared of God, a mind matured
and disciplined by action in difficult fields of thought,
and experience developed by varied contact with the
world, and a knowlege of business arrangement
acquired in the diversified functions of his secular
experience.

His wisdom and executive capacity in the office
were only equalled by his power to enlist attention
and awaken interest in behalf of his cause. With no
pretension to oratory, he went before the people in
the most humble way, presenting in a conversational
style his simple statement ; but, warming with the
deep interest of his theme, he grew eloquent, and
seldom closed without riveting his subject upon the
conscience, or moving his audience to tears.

He had wise and able counsellors in the Board and in the Executive Committee, and often the assistance of the most eloquent voices in the Church to commend his cause; but, during the whole thirty years of his incumbency, Walter Lowrie was himself the efficient head of the missionary work, and the controlling power in its administration.

I need scarcely indicate the results.

The cause of missions is securely established in the confidence and affection of the Church. Its policy is settled, its missionaries have gone forth to the ends of the earth—to the savages in our own wilderness, to India, Siam, China, Japan, Africa, South America, to the Papal countries of Europe, and to God's ancient people, the Jews.

With a success that might well compensate for a life of toil, with the ripe fruitage of his work before him, Walter Lowrie laid himself down to rest, and now sleeps in Jesus.

As we review his record and estimate his character, its first and leading feature is—Consecration, self-sacrificing consecration to the glory of God in the world's evangelization.

No one who knew him ever doubted that he had any chief aim but the glory of God, in the whole plan and action of his life. He had learned, by a deep experience, that he was not his own, but bought with a price; and therefore he sought to glorify God in his body and spirit. To this his consecration was *entire.* He could say with as much truth as Paul, "This one thing I do." No man ever devoted himself with a more entire concentration to any one work than did Walter Lowrie to the work of Missions. He gave to this one thing his whole heart, soul, mind and strength.

His devotion, too, was marked by SELF-SACRIFICE. He sacrificed political distinction, civil station, ease, emolument, personal preferment ; in a word, everything that the world calls gain, he counted loss for the glory of Christ in the work of missions.

He was never willing to receive in the way of salary as much as the Board was willing to give him. He used his private means first, and whatever more was necessary to meet his expenses, that much, and no more, would he receive in the way of compensation. For the last few years, if I mistake not, he declined receiving any salary whatever.

But his chief sacrifice was the surrender of his sons to labour, and some of them to die in the missionary field. His third son, Rev. Walter M. Lowrie, having caught from his father the spirit of zeal and consecration, was among the first missionaries who sailed to China under the care of the Presbyterian Board. After a short period of effective labour, he fell a martyr under the murderous hands of Chinese pirates on the 18th of August, 1847. "He was a man of eminent talents, an accomplished scholar, an able minister of the Gospel, and a faithful and devoted missionary."

His fourth son, Rev. Reuben Lowrie, who through all his early education had looked forward to an association with his brother in the missionary field, was happily prepared both by providence and grace to step forward and fill the place made vacant by the death of his lamented brother. But he also, after a short period of six years labour, fell a sacrifice to assiduous work and the enervating effect of an unpropitious climate. His brother missionaries speak of him as "a man of fine talent, earnest piety, sound scholarship and unwavering devotedness to the early-formed purpose of his life, even amid the ravages of disease."

His eldest son, Dr. John C. Lowrie, of whose earlier devotion to missions we have already spoken, as having drawn his father's heart into a closer sympathy with this great work, after a period of labour in India, was compelled to return with shattered health, but has since been engaged in the same work at home.

But, passing from these recitals of self-sacrifice, we may designate as a second marked characteristic of our lamented secretary—HIS ABIDING CONFIDENCE IN THE SUCCESS OF MISSIONS, AS FOUNDED UPON THE DIVINE PROMISE.

He evinced the deepest conviction of the perishing condition of the heathen, and of the necessity of the Gospel, not simply to ameliorate their condition, but as absolutely necessary to their salvation. Persuaded that the ascending Master had devolved upon the Church the duty of sending this Gospel as the appointed means of salvation into all the world, he never doubted for a moment its ultimate success. He went forward with the confidence of a man who knew God's purpose and who meant to fulfill it. He believed that the enthroned Mediator governs the world in the interest of His Church, and that, therefore, the kingdoms of this world shall become the kingdoms of our Lord and of His Christ.

In this confidence he walked by faith, and to him it was as clear an evidence as if he had beheld by sight the end for which he hoped.

A third feature of his life work is—THE PERSEVERING DILIGENCE WITH WHICH HE EMPLOYED MEANS FOR THE SUCCESS OF HIS UNDERTAKING.

His faith was no indolent repose in the Divine sovereignty and efficiency ; but a vigorous effort to obtain God's help, in the use of the means of His appointment.

He believed that as human hands must roll away the stone from the grave of Lazarus before Jesus called him to life, so human work must do what it can for the heathen, and when thus done, in believing expectation, Jesus will speak the word of power that will raise the dead. Hence all his plans contemplated *work*, diligent, persevering *work*. He worked himself, worked unceasingly, and expected others to be diligent, always abounding in the work of the Lord.

But the fourth and perhaps the chief distinction in our departed father was—THE CHARACTER OF HIS RELIGION. It was a religion of PRINCIPLE. He acted from a conviction of right and duty, and at the point of his conscience. He was never carried away by emotion. He had the tenderest sympathy for the suffering, and always melted when he spoke of the love of Jesus : but he never suffered his emotions to sway his judgment.

He was never influenced by excitement, or carried away from his position by epidemical impulses. He had a calm mind, a clear discrimination, a sagacity that perceived the truth amidst much mist and confusion, a judgment of men and things, cautious indeed, but certain in its conclusions, and therefore firm and persistent in their maintenance. It was this that made him a man of decision and will. His simple question was, What is truth, what is duty ? and when this was ascertained, he knew of no motives of policy or expediency to make him halt or swerve in his course of action.

It was this that gave him power. He was a man to mould circumstances, and not to be moulded by them. This is indeed the element of all true greatness. A goodly purpose, influenced by benevolent feeling, under the guidance of a clear judgment and a resistless will, forms the men who make their mark upon the age, and carry forward great enterprises to successful completion.

But time would fail to amplify further this review of his life and character.

He is gone, and we miss him—miss him not only in the Board, in which he was the presiding genius, but we miss him in this church of which he has been for so many years the beloved and venerated elder; miss him in the social circle of friends and acquaintances, who delighted to pay him reverence; miss him in his family, where he was the centre of interest and affection, and where, most of all, they mourn that he is not.

Many a heart is saddened by his departure; many a missionary family scattered over the earth will weep tears of sorrow when these tidings reach their distant homes.

But being dead, he yet speaketh.

He speaks to the Church—summoning it to carry on the work which he has begun; to stand by the Board, and by increased contributions to enable it, not only to sustain the labourers now in the field, but to carry forward the standard and place it upon the outmost wall.

He speaks to the Board—to the men who stood around him in the darker hours of the night, and says, as it were, "Brethren, be faithful unto death."

He speaks to the missionaries in the field—

encouraging them in the conflict with the powers of darkness. As the Scottish chief who had fallen in the battle, when he saw his lines waver, arose upon his elbow, and, as the blood poured from his wounds, exclaimed, "Children, I am not dead, I am with you still," so it would seem if our departed missionary chieftain was saying with his dying breath, "Children, I am with you still. Stand fast in the battle. Scale every wall. Pull down every stronghold, and let no man be wanting now, when the cry goes out, To the help of the Lord, to the help of the Lord against the mighty."